Viper Breed

Willie Brady is searching high and low for the capital to fulfil his lifelong ambition of running his own freight company. He's not having much luck, and his girlfriend, fearful of being left on the shelf, has had enough. So when Willie refuses to let her ask her brother for help, a public bust-up follows, during which Willie vows to get the money he needs one way or another.

But when the detective hired by Ashley Bryant, Oakville's richest man, to convey one hundred thousand dollars back east is robbed and murdered, the finger is pointed at Willie. With the perfect motive and an unlikely alibi Willie is in deep trouble.

As the evidence mounts up, it becomes a race against time to catch the real killer before Willie mounts the gallows himself.

By the same author

Gambler For Hire

Viper Breed

RIO BLANE

A Black Horse Western

ROBERT HALE · LONDON

First published in Great Britain 2002

ISBN 0 7090 7046 2

Robert Hale Limited
Clerkenwell House
Clerkenwell Green
London EC1R 0HT

Typeset by
Derek Doyle & Associates, Liverpool.
Printed and bound in Great Britain by
Antony Rowe Limited, Wiltshire

This one especially for Mike

ONE

'I reckon I'm a pretty good risk, sir.'

The president of the Oakville bank, struggling to shuck the weed, chewed on an unlit Havana, fiddled with his fob-chain that spread across his expanse of expensively clothed belly, never taking his eyes off the man sitting across the wide mahogany desk behind which he sat on a plush red chair, more akin to a throne than a chair.

The man sitting opposite, being more used to the hell-raising environs of a bunkhouse and the gregariousness of its inhabitants, was uneasy in the opulent surroundings of Andrew Benton's office, and somewhat in awe of the great man himself.

In fact, he felt as uncomfortable as a bank-robber under Benton's inscrutable gaze.

'You do, do you, Mr . . . ah?'

'Brady,' the tall, eager-eyed borrower supplied,

for the third time in a three-minute conversation. He swept back a tumble of fair hair that had formed a permanent fringe, feeling that his wind-blown appearance was not the kind of jib that would impress a bank president. He was now regretting not having worn the new suit he'd got for his cousin Louie's wedding in Montana a year ago. Lucy Webster had warned him to.

To make the right impression.

Lucy's words.

But, darn, he felt as trussed up as a Christmas turkey in street duds!

Lucy, as always, had got it right, if Andrew Benton's sniffing perusal of him was anything to judge by. 'Willie,' he tagged on. 'Willie Brady, sir.'

Andrew Benton did some more chewing on his cigar, before saying, 'A thousand dollars is a whole stack of money, son.'

'I guess,' Willie agreed.

'It wouldn't be easy to meet the repayments on such a sum,' Benton cautioned.

'No, sir. But with hard work and savvy, I reckon I can make a go of this freight company I have a hankerin' to start up.'

'Oakville already has a freighter in Charlie Webster; a mighty fine one at that. Got a shipment of fine china the other day, only three cups and two plates broken.'

Willie Brady boasted, 'Use the new Brady

Freight Company, and you'll get all your china intact, Mr Benton, sir.'

Andrew Benton chuckled. 'Well now, aren't you the cocky fella.' The bank president chewed on his Havana some more. 'Aren't you and Lucy Webster sweethearts?'

Willie felt hot colour rush to his face. 'We ain't, as you say, sweethearts, Mr Benton . . .'

'Oh? Last time I saw you two over in the Golden Plate eaterie, you looked real cosy in each other's company.' He smiled what Willie Brady thought was not an unkind smile. For a bank manager, that is. 'In fact you only had eyes for each other, young man.'

'We've walked out together a coupla times, yeah, sure. But sweethearts?' Willie sighed. 'Well that's a step we ain't taken yet.'

Andrew Benton set his cigar aside. He took a paper bag of boiled sweets from the desk drawer and took to sucking a cherry-red sweet. He offered the bag of sweets to Willie, but sweets were never his thing and he politely refused the banker's generosity.

'I suck some, to help me quit the weed,' said Benton. He held up the chewed cigar. 'Filthy habit!' Now, instead of sitting chewing, he sat sucking, while the seconds ticked by on the bank clock behind him; seconds that were as painful as the nails in the Saviour's hands to Willie Brady.

'A thousand dollars, huh?' Benton pondered.

'With an overdraft,' Willie added.

Benton's eyes shot open. 'Overdraft?'

Willie wondered if it might have been wiser to lay all his cards on the table right off, but he figured that first securing the thousand dollars he needed to start his freight company, before talking about initial running costs until he received payment for delivering his first couple of loads, was the smarter thing to do.

Lucy had said not. He should have listened to her. It looked like a cards on the table, dealt-in-street-duds approach, was the strategy he should have employed.

Benton frowned. 'How many cards have you got up that sleeve of yours, son?'

'Not much of an overdraft,' Willie hurriedly assured the banker. 'Getting a wagon and team will eat up most of the thousand dollars,' he explained. 'Then there'll be rent for the store over on Delancey Street. And of course—'

Andrew Benton sprang out of his plushly upholstered chair, hands raised as if he'd just been held up. 'Hold it right there, mister!' he commanded.

The second Willie Brady walked into the Golden Plate, where he'd arranged to meet Lucy Webster for lunch, his hangdog look told her that there would be no discussion of plans to set up the Brady Freight Company and, more importantly, her trip up the aisle! Her spirits slumped.

'Benton slung me out on my ear,' Willie groaned.

Lucy's glance was critical.

'Can't say that I blame him, Willie Brady. You look like something the cat dragged in; something really unpleasant, too!'

Willie consciously slapped the range dust from his clothes with his hat. 'Told you I itch somethin' awful in street duds, Lucy.'

'Oh, sit down,' she said. 'You're making yourself conspicuous, and me look a fool, Willie Brady!' Dejected, Willie slipped on to a chair, hunkering down to make himself as out of view as was possible in the busy cafe. Lucy's anger faded and she took Willie's hands in hers.

'It isn't fair,' she proclaimed. 'I'll have a talk with Charlie right away. He'll have a word with Benton, and—'

'No, Lucy,' Willie emphatically stated. 'I'll set up the Brady Freight Company on my own, or I won't do it at all!'

'Why, that's silly, and plain stubborn too. No man's above getting help now and then, Willie. Charlie—'

'No, Lucy,' Willie interjected hotly. 'Like I said—'

'I know.' Despondent, she sighed. 'You'll set up Brady Freight without anyone's charity.'

'Don't be mad at me, Lucy,' he pleaded. 'You gotta understand that it's important to a man to be able to do for himself.'

Frustrated, she pleaded in return, 'I know that, Willie. But how in heck are we ever going to get to walking out, if you won't accept help?'

' 'Nother coupla years cow-punchin' should do it.'

'A couple of years?' Lucy Webster wailed. 'I'm twenty-two, Willie. If I'm not hitched in another year, then I'm surely on the shelf for my natural.'

'That ain't so, Lucy. Why, over in Lark Creek only last summer, a woman of twenty-six got hitched. Mary Belle Ryan, she was.'

'Twenty-six?' Lucy asked, goggle-eyed.

'And maybe some more, too,' Willie huddled close in a confidential whisper. ' 'Cause those Ryans are Irish. So help me, each one a bigger and better liar than the other! They tell stories so tall they reach into the clouds.'

Lucy shook her auburn head in wonder, her brown eyes even wider still. 'Twenty-six!'

'So, you see,' Willie consoled her. 'Twenty-two ain't so darn terrible as you think.'

Suddenly, Lucy Webster's despondency was back with a bang.

'Yeah. But I was only sixteen yesterday, Willie.'

'Huh?'

'Time takes no time at all to pass. All you've got saved is two hundred dollars, and that took three years to get together. Now, if it takes three years to save two hundred dollars, how long will it take to save a thousand?' Lucy's lips moved in a mental calculation, and on reaching the answer she paled. 'Fifteen years, Willie!'

The other diners in the restaurant paused, all eyes going Willie and Lucy's way.

'Shush, Lucy,' Willie pleaded.

'Shush,' she whined. 'I'll be fit for burying before—'

Angered by Lucy's insistence on making a scene, Willie Brady hotly declared loudly, 'I'll have the Brady Freight Company up and runnin' 'fore you know it, honey.'

'How?' she quizzed him. Both were oblivious now to the other diners' uninhibited interest in their conversation.

'Dunno, yet. But I'll find a way. You just be patient a little longer.'

'Willie Brady,' Lucy Webster trumpeted, 'my patience with you is at an end. I'm going to find me a man of substance. I'm gathering dust on the shelf. You'll never be anything other than a cow-sitter!'

Willie became aware of Ashley Bryant, Oakville's richest man, with a finger in every pie in town including a share in Webster Freight, enjoying every second of his humiliation. Bryant, like most men in Oakville, would not hesitate to take Lucy Webster off the shelf she imagined herself to be on.

Lucy stood up and pulled herself up to her full, pert, five foot five inches and primly declared, 'I'd appreciate it if you did not bother me again, Mr Brady.'

'You wait and see, Lucy,' Willie angrily shouted after her. 'I'll have Brady Freight up and runnin' in no time at all.'

Lucy swung around, her eyes stormy. 'And there'll be white blackbirds too, Willie Brady!'

Willie, throwing all caution to the wind, challenged the patrons of the Golden Plate café. 'Well, what're ya all gawkin' at?'

Ashley Bryant sniggered. 'You know, Brady. You haven't got the spit in you for such a feisty filly as Lucy Webster. I might just pay my respects to Lucy myself.'

'Do and you'll be eatin' my fist!' Willie snarled, and stormed out of the Golden Plate.

'My, oh my. There goes a real angry fella,' Bryant opined.

Crashing through the Golden Plate door, head down and growling, Willie knocked heads with Saul Jackson, Oakville's marshal.

'Hold up there, young Willie,' the marshal said

in a friendly tone, massaging his forehead. 'What's got a normally easy-going fella like you so het up?'

'Sorry, Marshal Jackson,' Willie apologized. 'Some days are just bad, ain't that so?'

'Real stinkers,' Jackson drawled in his easy way. His glance followed the equally sparking Lucy Webster sashaying along the boardwalk, raising every man's blood pressure. 'Looks like it's a bad day for more'n one citizen, too?'

Jackson looked at Willie with the shrewd grey eyes which, over the years, had unnerved many a hardcase.

'No loan for that freight line you've got your heart on starting up, huh, son?'

Piqued, Willie declared, 'Darn it. Ain't a man got a right to his own business in this burg?'

'Settle down, Willie,' the marshal advised. 'It isn't a secret what your hankering is. So, when you're seen going into the bank, and then coming out with a face that would frighten Satan . . . Well, it isn't hard to put two and two together, now is it son?'

'I guess not, Marshal Jackson,' Willie conceded, the steam gone out of him. 'But like I just told Lucy. I'm goin' to start that freight company, come hell or high water.'

'You won't do anything foolish, will you?' Jackson cautioned.

Willie was forced to step aside to allow Ashley Bryant and two of his cronies, who were leaving the Golden Plate, to pass.

'I hope you know what you're doing, entrusting all that money to a stranger,' one of Bryant's cronies was saying to the financier and mortgage lender.

'Don't have a choice, gents,' Bryant said. 'This blue-chip stock won't be around for ever, and I need to get cash to Boston right away to close the deal.'

'Ever heard of banks, Ashley?' the second man with Oakville's richest man asked.

Jackson concluded that the man must be a new acquaintance of Bryant's. Otherwise he would have known of the mortgage lender's distrust of banks. When he was a young man he had entrusted his first one hundred dollars to a bank. One morning when he had called at the opening of business, the bank safe had been cleaned out of every cent, the banker long gone.

'Good morning, Marshal.'

'Mr Bryant,' Jackson replied, touching his hat.

'Don't doff your hat to that rat!' Willie raged.

Bryant paused, his sneer goading Willie. 'Gents,' he told his friends, 'if you've got any freight to shift, Mr Brady here will be glad to oblige.' His sneer deepened. 'That is, if you can wait a spell.' He swaggered past. 'Looks like the

Brady Freight Company is going to take a while to get going.'

His smug friends joined in Ashley Bryant's mocking laughter. Saul Jackson stepped in front of Willie to block his path to Bryant.

'It'll be up and runnin' in no time at all. You'll see!' Brady hollered.

'My advice,' Bryant said, 'is for you to stick to punching cows, and not get in above your head in business, Brady.'

'I won't always be a cow-puncher,' Brady vowed.

Bryant laughed. 'Doesn't look like you'll be a freighter either.'

Bryant and his friends strolled on, shoulders shaking with new laughter.

'I'll be a damn freighter, you'll see!' Willie shouted after Bryant. 'You'll see,' he said in a quieter tone.

'If I were you I'd rein in that temper, Willie. It could get you in a whole mess of trouble if you don't,' the marshal said.

Willie Brady's shoulders slumped. 'How much more trouble can I be in, Marshal Jackson? With Lucy having just kicked me out of her life. No trouble could be worse than that. I'd just about do anythin' to win her back.'

'Lucy Webster is a sensible young woman. She'll come round,' said Jackson. He smiled. 'Lord knows how you two will live together though. With the hellish tempers you've both got.'

The marshal shoved Willie ahead of him to his hitched horse.

'Meantime, you've got work to do back at the Broken Wheel. If I know Luke Harper, the old skinflint will be sweating drops of blood every second that you're not foraging for your keep. Now, git!'

Jackson had made light of Brady's time away from the Broken Wheel, but in reality Luke Harper was indeed sweating blood trying to hold on to the ranch which he had built up from the first blade of grass to one of the finest spreads in the territory. But a wastrel son, a dry season, and a blood-sucking mortgage from Ashley Bryant had left Harper in a bind. He had confided to Jackson, an old friend, that he had his hands full in keeping the Broken Wheel from going under.

Harper, already heavily in debt to the bank, was finding the additional burden of Bryant's exhorbitant interest rates more than he could cope with. Bryant had had a greedy eye on the Broken Wheel for a long time. It was no secret that he hoped to square Harper's loan with the bank. Then with no other interested party in the reckoning, he planned on foreclosing on Harper.

Andrew Benton, the bank president, knew of Ashley Bryant's conniving scheme and had, up to now, stalled his efforts to pick up Luke Harper's loan with the bank. But Benton could not hold out for ever. The bank had shareholders and its customers' well-being to think of. Jackson reckoned that sooner than later Andrew Benton's hand would be forced, and he'd have to accept Bryant's offer.

To add to Luke Harper's woes, Jesse, his son and his hope for the future of the Broken Wheel, spent most of his time running up gambling and boozing debts at the Happy Lizard saloon in Oakville – an Ashley Bryant establishment! Where Jesse Harper was being given unlimited credit.

'You being the law, ain't there somethin' you can do about Jesse, Saul?' Luke Harper had pleaded with the marshal.

Anxious to help one of his oldest friends, Jackson had spoken to Ashley Bryant about him giving Jesse Harper free access to his gambling tables, bar and whores, but had come away with his tail firmly between his legs. Bryant had rightly told him that he would do what he liked with his own money. And if he wanted to indulge Jesse Harper, then that was his prerogative.

'Jesse is going to ruin me for sure,' the rancher had confided to the marshal, 'if that devil Ashley Bryant isn't roped in.'

'Ain't much I can do, Luke,' Jackson had told

Harper. 'Ashley Bryant is a legitimate businessman.'

'Legitimate businessman my foot!' Luke Harper had railed. 'Bryant's as curly as a pig's tail!' The rancher's fiery eyes had locked with Jackson's. 'And you know it, too, Saul.'

He had admitted to his suspicions of Harper's claims.

Resignedly, the rancher had said, 'I damn well know. He's bleeding me dry with that loan I had the stupidity to rope myself into.'

Jackson had said, 'You'll have to get Jesse in line, Luke. You know that.' Sternly he had warned, 'I've been turning a blind eye to his antics in town. But I'm running out of excuses that folk will believe. Sooner or later I'm going to have to bring Jesse to book, if he doesn't change his ways.'

'He ain't done anything really bad, Saul,' Harper had defended. 'Jesse is a little wild, but he ain't the first wild one 'round here.'

'And he won't be the last, Luke. But no one's got as much rope from me as Jesse has.'

Luke Harper had agreed. 'I'll take him aside, Saul. Straighten him out.'

'I'm counting on you doing just that, Luke,' Jackson had warned.

Then the rancher had complained to the marshal. 'Why the hell can't Jesse be as level-headed as Willie Brady? Willie will make a fine man.' He sighed wearily. 'The kind of man that the Broken Wheel will need to survive in the future, Saul.'

Luke Harper had gone on to reveal more of his thoughts.

'Willie would make one fine go of the Broken Wheel; make it even better than it is right now.' The rancher's eyes clouded over with worry. 'Hell, that ain't much. Willie would make it better than it ever was, I reckon.'

Harper's lavish praise of Willie Brady had come as a surprise to Jackson. Willie had worked for the Broken Wheel since he'd been twelve years old, having had to become an earner when his father had been kicked in the gut by a rogue plough-horse. He'd kept the roof over the head of his ailing mother who, after Sam Brady's death had withdrawn into herself, hardly ever speaking again between then and when she had died when Willie was fourteen.

Luke Harper, a decent and Christian man, had paid Willie over the going rate for the little he could contribute to the smooth running of the ranch, as a charity to Eloise Brady whom he had looked on for a time as a replacement for his late wife, Mary. But Eloise Brady had lived her remaining days giving over every second to thinking about Sam Brady, not letting another man near her, until her thoughts had sucked the life from her. When she died, Luke Harper took Willie into his home, and had treated him equally with his own son Jesse.

But no one knew, up to a minute before when he had trumpeted Willie Brady's virtues to the marshal, how kindly and lovingly he looked on Willie.

Being a private man himself, Saul Jackson was slow to pry into another man's thoughts. And as his old friend was not forthcoming beyond what he'd already said, the matter had rested there.

With only a year between them, Willie Brady being the senior, he and Jesse Harper had become like brothers, except when it came to Lucy Webster, when the sparks flew between them. And Lucy, engaging in typical female antics, had often had the boys at each other's throats for her favour. A couple of months before, when Lucy had finally come down in favour of Willie, Jesse Harper had taken her decision in good faith.

Or had he?

It was about that time that his visits to the Happy Lizard had become more frequent and more troublesome. At that second, Marshal Jackson's reverie was interrupted by one such outburst.

TWO

The window of the Happy Lizard disintegrated under a bullet, and as it crashed on to the street, Saul Jackson could see a swaying Jesse Harper, six-gun in hand, stagger around the saloon, holding the pistol on a lanky gent who had ridden into town the day before, and had earned the marshal's scrutiny to the point where Jackson had searched through his stack of dodgers. His search had proved futile, the stranger was not wanted. Or at least, if he was, word had not reached Oakville yet.

'You spilled it. You lick it up, mister!' Jesse Harper ranted.

'You bumped into me,' the lanky man said, in a no-nonsense tone. 'If you want it, you lick it up.'

A doe-eyed saloon dove by the name of Lil Scannell, almost constantly on Jesse Harper's arm, tried to intervene in the bad-tempered fracas, but Harper shoved her aside. On her second attempt to talk sense to the rancher's son, he fisted her in the face.

'Stay out of it, Willie!' Jackson warned, as Brady dismounted from the horse he had just mounted a couple of seconds before.

'Jesse will listen to me, Marshal,' Brady said.

'I doubt if he's of a frame of mind to listen to anyone right now, son,' Jackson opined.

'Who is that fella who's riled Jesse, anyway?' Willie wanted to know.

'Never saw his dial before,' the marshal answered. 'But I sure don't like the way he wears that thonged .45.'

'He ain't a gunfighter is he, Marshal?' Willie panicked.

'Dunno,' the Oakville lawman replied shortly. 'But I'm hoping he isn't.'

Willie grabbed the Winchester from his saddle scabbard. 'I'll cover you, Marshal.'

'Appreciate the gesture, Willie. But whatever happens, don't you go getting your fool head shot off, you hear.'

Brady hunched down by the side of the shattered saloon-window. 'Sure won't,' he promised, ''Cause me and Lucy Webster's goin' to have a whole lot of smoochin' to get through once she shucks that awful bout of tantrum she's in presently.'

Despite his problems, Saul Jackson laughed. 'In that case, Willie,' he humorously advised, 'don't stand up to do your shooting, if needs be.'

'Huh?' Willie enquired vaguely. And just as Marshal Jackson went through the bat-wings of the Happy Lizard, he chuckled. 'See what you mean, Marshal.'

'I said lick that damn beer off the floor, mister!' Jesse Harper screamed, his anger getting hotter by the second.

Jackson said, 'Put the gun down, Jesse.'

Harper swung around, his eyes aflame with temper. 'I can sort out my own problems, Marshal,' he grated.

Saul Jackson looked to the man whom Jesse Harper had challenged. The lanky stranger cast funeral eyes back at him. Jackson shivered. In that moment he had no doubt that both he and Harper would be harp-players if the man reacted to Jesse Harper's goading.

There was something about the man that spelled death.

'Ease back, Jesse,' the marshal advised.

'Good advice, Marshal,' the stranger intoned, his voice echoing up from hollow innards by the sound of it. 'Take it, son,' he advised Harper.

Jesse Harper, true to form of late, scoffed at the stranger's offer. 'Lick my boots, or use that iron,' he snarled.

The funeral-eyed stranger said, 'He's pushing, Marshal. Pushing more than a man has a right to suffer, wouldn't you say, sir?'

Though not a cowardly man, Saul Jackson experienced fear in the situation he found himself in.

'I won't condone a gunfight in my town, mister,' he told the lanky stranger. ''Sides, I reckon this contest is a mite mismatched.' He settled his gaze on the stranger. 'Wouldn't you say, sir?'

The stranger laughed. 'Mighty uneven, I'd say, Marshal,' he admitted.

'Then walk away,' said Jackson.

'Shut your gob!' Jesse Harper raged at the lawman. 'This crow-bait bastard isn't budging before he licks my damn boots.'

The lanky stranger shrugged. 'I reckon this ruckus is not going away, Marshal.'

'Yes it is!' the lawman pronounced grimly.

His fist swept up to land on Jesse Harper's jaw. The rancher's son spun backwards against the bar, smashing several tables on his way. Jackson watched thankfully as his six-gun catapulted from his grasp as he collided with the bar, clattering over it and behind it, out of reach.

The marshal quickly followed through, taking up a balled-fist stance in front of Harper, ready to finish what he'd begun if the young man decided to further pursue his gripe with the stranger.

'It's over, Jesse,' said Jackson. He ordered the barkeep, 'Get his head in a bucket of cold water and his belly full of coffee. Then go home,' he told the rancher's son sternly. 'You've put enough grey hairs on your pa's head.'

'Fast,' the stranger opined, a comment on Jackson's quick-flying fists. 'Drink, Marshal?'

'I figure you should be leaving town about now, mister,' Jackson stated grimly.

The lanky man leaned on the bar, taking up a comfortable stance that hinted at a long stay.

'Now, Marshal, I don't see any reason why you should run me out of town. Our young friend made all the running in this affair. He bumped into me and spilled his beer; not the other way round. Beer and bullets aren't a good combination, as you well know.'

Jackson said, 'I'm not placing blame, mister. I'm just removing temptation.'

The stranger sipped at his beer. The seconds ticking by on the wall-clock behind the bar had the boom of a blacksmith's hammer on an anvil. The lanky stranger left it to Jackson to break the dragging silence.

'You leaving?'

The man looked at the marshal's reflection in the mirror behind the bar. He sipped some more, before answering, 'I reckon I'll finish my beer first?'

Relieved, Jackson said, 'Sounds reasonable.'

Coming out of his stupor, Jesse Harper railed, 'You sucking up to this bastard, Jackson?'

Jackson said, 'Settle down, Jesse.' And to the stranger: 'You going to take long to finish that beer?'

The stranger gulped down the remains of his drink in one long slug.

'Obliged,' Jackson said.

Passing on his way to the door, the funeral-eyed stranger opined, 'That young fella isn't going to be around for long, I figure, Marshal.' He then added with menace, 'If you hadn't stepped in, he wouldn't be around right now.'

His senses rattled by pride, Jesse Harper grabbed the shotgun under the counter and vaulted over the bar.

Willie Brady's call was clarion clear. 'Duck, Marshal!'

As he dived to the floor, the shotgun-blast thundered over Saul Jackson's head. The stranger had thrown himself sideways, his gun arcing upwards to find Harper.

Willie Brady's rifle cracked. Jesse Harper howled. The shotgun slipped from his grasp, his hand shocked by the shoulder-nick Willie had inflicted. Brady's rifle cracked again, and a chunk of wood from the floor spun up at the stranger, forcing him to lean back out of its deadly path, throwing him off balance and giving Willie time to crash through the saloon bat-wings, his Winchester tracking any further trouble.

'You OK, Marshal?' he asked.

'I'm still sucking air thanks to you, Willie,' the lawman said, shaken by Jesse Harper's treachery.

He was on his way to lay in to the rancher's son when Willie stepped in front of him and swore, 'Damn it! Is this ruckus never goin' to end?'

Saul Jackson fought for control over his anger. Eventually regaining his composure, he agreed. 'You're right Willie. It's time to bring this shindig to an end.'

'Anyone asking my opinion?'

Jackson and Brady swung round to face the stranger.

'I'd prefer if you kept it to yourself, mister,' Jackson growled.

Ashley Bryant charged in. His immediate question was, 'Who's going to pay for all this damage?'

'Oh, go stick your head in a bucket, Ashley Bryant,' said Willie Brady. 'You're dancing about like one of those ballerinas in the pictures that Doc Flatley's missus brought back from her trip back East!'

In Willie Brady's opinion, Ashley Bryant

fussed and fumed in a way that a man should not.

'Get out,' the financier screamed. 'All of you!'

The man dressed in city duds and derby, who had entered with Bryant, stood off, caught between the mortgage-lender's antics and the threat of menace still lingering in the air.

'Mr Jasper,' Ashley Bryant addressed the man haughtily, 'let us return to my office to complete our business transaction. You'll want to be on your way as soon as possible.'

'Ach, aye, Mr Bryant, sir.'

'That the fella takin' Bryant's money back East?' Willie enquired of Jackson.

'That's him,' the marshal confirmed.

'Don't look to me that he could safely cross the road,' Willie opined.

'Don't be fooled,' said Jackson. 'Henry Jasper is one of the Pinkerton Agency's ace operatives.'

'Yeah?' Willie Brady was unimpressed. 'Well, seems kinda foolish, leastways to me, for Ashley Bryant to hand over a bundle of dollars to that,' he chuckled, 'jasper.'

'As I hear it, the desperadoes who've tangled with Henry Jasper wouldn't agree with you, Willie,' said the marshal. 'Henry Jasper's left a whole lot of busted skulls on the trails he's ridden.'

Willie Brady remained unconvinced. 'Talks kinda funny, don't he?'

'He's a Scot. Used to be what the English call a *bobby*.'

'A what?'

'An English constable, Willie.'

Willie Brady scratched his head. 'Thought you said he was a Scot, Marshal? Ain't that a different country?'

Saul Jackson chuckled. 'Well now, Willie. That's something that Englishmen and Scotsmen have jawed about for a long time. And I'm not going to confuse the issue further by adding my cent's worth to the debate.'

Willie Brady went to peer over the bat-wings after the departing Pinkerton detective, and reaffirmed his view. 'That Jasper fella still don't look like much to me, Marshal. If you ask me, Ashley is handin' over his dollars to a man who could be easily waylaid.'

Saul Jackson said, 'Well now, Willie. If you're thinking of tangling with Henry Jasper, you'd better creep instead of facing him up front. Draws a mean iron, I'm told.'

'Looks like a washpole dudded up to me!' snorted Willie.

'Yeah,' Jackson agreed. 'I guess maybe that's the mistake most fellas make, before tangling with Jasper. Too late to find out how mistaken they've been when they're hauling themselves off the floor.'

'Creep up, huh,' Willie Brady mumbled, thoughtfully.

Jackson turned to address the lanky stranger with whom Jesse Harper had tangled, but in the confusion he had slipped away.

Willie said, with no small amount of cockiness, 'Well, Marshal. If you think you can now manage on your own, I'll mosey on back to the Broken Wheel. Do those chores waitin' for me.' Striding out of the saloon be declared, 'Dang! Sometimes I think that I'm the only fella workin' on that ranch.' He paused in the bat-wings to ask, 'You comin', Jesse?'

The rancher's son, still clutching his nicked arm, was in a snarling mood. 'No I ain't.' He pulled the dove he'd discarded only minutes before to him, and kissed her with more viciousness than passion. 'I've got me man's work to do yet.' He dragged the dove with him. He turned mid-point on the stairs to fling back at Willie, 'You go on back to the ranch and suck up to Pa, the way you always have.'

Angered, Willie Brady flung back, 'The problem with you, Jesse, is that you don't know the diff'rence 'tween showin' respect and suckin' up!'

Jesse Harper snorted and continued upstairs.

Brady fretted, 'I don't know, should I leave him behind, Marshal Jackson? Mebbe I should dent his skull and sling him over my shoulder.'

'Leave him be, Willie,' was Jackson's advice. 'The humour Jesse is in right now, he'd be likely to go for iron. I'll keep an eye on him. Send him home when he sobers up.'

Willie's worry deepened. 'What if he challenges that stranger again?'

Jackson opined, 'Whatever else, Jesse is no fool. He knows in his heart that he's lucky to still have a pumping heart in his chest. I reckon he'll give the stranger a wide berth.'

'Sure hope you've got that right, Marshal,' Willie sighed. 'Anyways, I'd best be makin' tracks.'

As they strolled companionably to Brady's horse, Jackson said, 'Sorry you didn't raise the loan you need to start up that freight-hauling business you're so keen on, Willie.'

'But I ain't givin' up. No, sir. Not me.' As he swung into the saddle, Willie vowed, 'I'm goin' to get my hands on start-up cash by hook or crook, Marshal Jackson.'

Saul Jackson watched the young man ride off, full of admiration for the kind of sterling citizen he was sure Willie Brady would make; the kind of citizen Oakville needed more of. The marshal had known Willie since he was a nipper. Willie had even lived with him and his wife Martha for a couple of months after his ma's death, before Luke Harper had taken him under his wing at the Broken Wheel.

Willie had been the Bradys' only child, and folk wondered how two such healthy people as Eloise and Sam Brady had only managed one sprout.

'Damn, Sam must be sleepin' in the barn,' one town wag had joked, for which he'd earned Saul Jackson's fist in his smart-alec gob. The marshal and his wife Martha being childless, the wag's humour was the kind which Jackson took exception to.

Martha Jackson had pleaded with him to rear Willie as their own child. However, being a lawman in times when lead flew almost daily in Oakville, Jackson feared that Willie would end up an orphan for the second time. He also worried that, Martha being a sickly woman, she would find the high-spirited youngster too much to cope with. Luke Harper could, and did, provide security for Willie, and had done a fine job of rearing the boy. Much more so than he had his own son, Jesse.

Saul Jackson had often, over the years, regretted not having listened to his wife's pleading to take Willie Brady as their boy. A man could hold his head up proudly having a son of such sterling quality and uprightness. He had been lucky in his years as a lawman, having had a couple of close calls, but, other than suffering a shoulder wound in one bust-up, he had come through Oakville's turbulent times pretty much in fine fettle and was now looking forward, in a year or so, to a healthy retirement.

He could not have given Willie as much as Luke Harper had given him, like those trips back east for example. But he took pride in the knowledge that Willie held him in high esteem, and would have been happy as his and Martha's son.

Feeling eyes on his back, a sense that had served him well in his years as marshal, Jackson swung around to see Jesse Harper glaring down on him from a bedroom window in the Happy Lizard. It pained him to be on the receiving end of such a malevolent glare. It ached his heart to see his friend's boy go bad, but bad he now truly was, constantly seeking trouble and wanting to use a gun to fix it with.

Sadly, if Jesse Harper did not change his ways soon, he'd be occupying a plot in the town cemetery before he grew much older. In recent times he had stepped in to extricate the rancher's son from potentially lethal confrontations. The ruckus he'd just been through, in which Willie Brady had played no small part in saving his and Jesse's hides, had been Harper's third brush with danger in as many weeks. And of the three, it had been his luckiest escape yet. Saul Jackson had no doubt that had the lanky stranger whom Jesse had faced down taken a more malicious stance in dealing with his challenge, the heir to the Broken

Wheel would now be lying in Mort Bellings' funeral parlour, instead of staring at him.

Lil Scannell, the doe-eyed whore who was Jesse Harper's current favourite among the Happy Lizard pleasure-pack, joined him at the window. Jesse whispered in her ear, while all the time keeping his eyes on Jackson. Then the two of them burst in to belly-shaking laughter, their faces ripe with lewdness.

The marshal knew the joke was on him, the way the dove's eyes shot his way as Harper's whispering ended. They vanished from the window. The marshal shucked his urge to walk right into the Happy Lizard and sink a fist in Jesse Harper's face. He'd let the rancher's son be; let him take his pleasure. That way it might be easier to persuade him to go on home.

Wearily, Saul Jackson made his way to the marshal's office, knowing that soon, and very soon he reckoned, he'd have to face up to Jesse Harper. It wasn't doing his pride any good to keep backing off the way he had been doing. It encouraged other troublemakers. The badge he wore made him the protector of all of Oakville's citizens, and not the minder of just one.

The Fall day had become overcast, its light grey and gloomy. On reaching the law office, and facing a backlog of paperwork, (his crib these days being that a lawman needed a fine nib instead of a fast gun to deal with the paperwork of the bureaucracy that had sprung up with the coming of more formal law and order) Jackson scratched a lucifer on his boot-heel and put it to the lamp-wick. Well soaked, it flared instantly, its yellow light dancing on the walls.

'Was that Willie Brady who stepped in to help you just now, Marshal?'

Startled and angry that his visitor should have got the drop on him, the lawman swung around to face the lanky stranger from the saloon seated behind the door.

'What business would that be of yours, mister?' he growled.

'Is he Willie Brady?' the stranger pressed.

'Yeah. That was Willie, all right. Now why're you asking? And who the hell are you, mister?'

The information requested in Jackson's last question was readily given.

'The name's Boothroyd.'

The hairs on the back of Jackson's neck curled.

'Hank Boothroyd, Marshal.'

Now the hairs stood on end, and Jackson's blood rushed to his feet.

The gaunt-faced visitor rubbed a bony hand along his pointed chin. His grey gaze remained on the marshal, seeing into his soul.

'You like Willie, don't you, Marshal?'

'I'd be proud to have him as my boy. In fact he

almost was.'

'You sound regretful that he isn't?'

'That I am, sir,' Saul Jackson admitted.

Hank Boothroyd became thoughtful. Then, after a long silent spell, he said, 'I hope you're ready for this, Marshal Jackson . . .'

THREE

Jackson was not.

'Kind of hits you a hammer-whack, doesn't it?' said Boothroyd. 'But it's true.'

Jackson shook his head, trying to take in the secret that Hank Boothroyd had revealed to him.

'You go blabbering before the time is right,' Boothroyd warned the marshal matter-of-factly, 'I'll kill you.' His tone dropped a notch to chill Saul Jackson's marrow. 'Just like I would have that pushy youngster just now, only for Willie putting in an appearance.'

Jackson closely studied the gunfighter's lean, hawkish face, and said, 'I don't take kindly to threats, Mr Boothroyd.'

Hank Boothroyd considered Jackson for a long moment. 'Didn't expect you would, Marshal.' The gunfighter strolled casually to the door. 'Thing is, you know that you haven't got the gun-skill necessary to outdraw me.'

Jackson knew that, so far, no man had had that prowess or luck.

'Be seeing you, Marshal.'

When Boothroyd left, Saul Jackson leaned on the desk to overcome the weakness in his legs. He reckoned that he was not the first lawman who had had such an experience on coming face to face with one of the West's deadliest, yet less well known gunfighters. Hank Boothroyd followed his profession quietly, not seeking the headlines which his contemporaries sought; contemporaries who gave Hank Boothroyd a wide berth when he entered their territory.

'Damn!' Saul Jackson swore. 'Looks like Oakville's set to become a hotbed of trouble!'

'You interested or not, Jesse Harper?' Lil Scannell, the raven-haired saloon dove, groused, as Harper rolled away from her to the other side of the bed. 'Don't do a girl's ego no good the way you're moonin' 'bout.'

'Oh, hush your griping!' he snarled, and laid a hand across the whore's face. The room filled with the crack of the vicious blow. He leapt from the bed and began pacing the room, oblivious to his nakedness.

'Why'd ya do that, honey?' Lil whined. 'You know I love ya.'

'Hah!' Jesse scoffed. 'What you love, Lil Scannell, is my poke, not my stroke!'

'But, Jesse honey—'

'Shut up!' he interjected, spitefully. 'Want the other side of your ugly dial hammered?' He resumed his agitated pacing. 'I got thinking to do, woman.'

'What about, Jesse?'

'About how belly-sick I am of my old man's grousing, and this shithole burg that I had the godawful misfortune to be born in.' Grimly, he pronounced, 'I'm planning on shucking this dump, Lil.'

Enthused by Harper's statement, seeing herself as part of Jesse Harper's long-term plans, Lil Scannell began making suggestions as to where they might head for, ending dreamily with her favourite.

'New Orleans. Now there's the town for us, Jesse.'

He laughed harshly and mockingly. 'You're not going to hog my heels, you broken-down whore!'

Stung, Lil pleaded, 'But you always said—'

'Oh, shit, Lil.' He laughed derisively. 'You didn't believe me, did you?' His grin was cruel. 'I only told you that so as you'd do that little trick I like so much, and you hate so much.'

Lil, belittled and defeated, sprang at Jesse with claws as damaging as any mountain cat's. Harper howled as her nails tore at his back. Rage-driven, he took to beating the dove, raining in one vicious blow after another. He threw her across the room and, too weak to control her headlong dive, Lil Scannell crashed through the bedroom window. Her scream followed her down on to the street.

Jackson, still pondering on Hank Boothroyd's secret, leapt out of his chair on hearing Lil Scannell's heart-rending scream.

'What the blazes . . .?'

He stormed out of the law office and hurried along to where a crowd was gathering, their glances switching between the shattered saloon-window and the focus of their attention on the street.

'Step aside,' Jackson ordered authoritatively. Pushing his way through the crowd, he came up short on seeing the saloon dove's mangled condition, her raven hair blood-streaked.

'Came right through that window, Marshal,' a small, bow-legged man told him. 'Seen it. Came right through and fell like a damn sack o' 'taters.'

Lil moaned pitifully.

'Someone go fetch Doc Flatley,' the marshal instructed. 'Tell him to get here fast.'

A tall, loose-limbed man broke from the crowd

and began a loping run towards the far end of Main to Flatley's infirmary.

Jackson, a believer in what you sowed you reaped, was, nevertheless, moved by compassion. He went on one knee and gently cradled the broken saloon dove in his arms. 'You hang in there, Lil. Doc's on his way.'

After a moment, he handed over the task of comforting the whore to another man. His gaze became fixed on the shattered upstairs window of the Happy Lizard. Grimly, he set out for the saloon.

Quick-witted as a fox, Jesse Harper hightailed it along the hall to the room of another dove who was Lil Scannell's rival for his company, just as Saul Jackson's footsteps pounded upstairs. Harper slipped into Conchita Murales's shaded bedroom, her present client preferring the blinds drawn. The rancher's son was in luck. The Mexican whore's customer was a Broken Wheel ranny. Harper shoved a wad of dollar bills in the ranny's fist, threw him his clothes and warned him, 'I've been here with Conchita all the time. You understand, Danny?'

The ranny, quick on the uptake, smiled. 'Sure, Jesse.' He checked the dollars in his mitt, and his grin widened considerably. 'I'll even swear to that m'self.'

'How much you geeve him?' Conchita asked Harper, seeing an opportunity for profit.

Trapped and not liking it, Jesse Harper growled, 'Don't worry. You'll get the same.'

'Now, Jesse honey,' Conchita demanded, holding out her hand. 'Lying don't come cheep, eh, Jesse baby.'

'I'm not a walking bank,' snapped Harper. 'My word is good, isn't it?'

Conchita Murales considered this for a moment, and then, with a toothy smile, flung back the bedclothes. 'It ees true, what you say, Jesse honey.'

Harper jumped into bed. Conchita looked from the ranny to Harper and laughed. 'I pleese you both, eh.'

Danny sighed. 'Heck, I've died and gone to heaven!' The Broken Wheel ranny looked hopefully at Jesse.

'Yeah,' the rancher's son said grudgingly. 'You can keep the money.'

Marshal Jackson angrily kicked in the door of the room from where he had seen Harper and Lil Scannell watching him a short time before. The room was empty. He stepped back out to the hall and hollered, 'Jesse . . . Jesse Harper!'

In Conchita's room, the rancher's son unwillingly got out of bed, Conchita proving to be a woman of many tricks. 'Remember,' he told the Mexican whore and the Broken Wheel ranny. 'This has been a threesome for a spell.'

He went to the room door and eased it open, ruffling his hair before he did so. Stepping into the hall, he asked, 'What's all the hollering about, Marshal?'

'You're under arrest, Jesse,' Jackson declared.

'Arrest, Marshal Jackson?' His wide-eyed innocence showed how good an actor he was. 'What for?' He chuckled easily. 'I ain't done nothin', unless showing Conchita what a real man looks like is a crime in this town now.'

'Right now for assault,' the marshal said, in answer to his first question. 'Likely murder though.'

'Murder?'

'Lil Scannell is in pretty bad shape, Jesse.' He shook his head in disgust. 'Never had any time for a woman-beater. Get dressed.'

Jesse Harper's sneer raised Jackson's hackles enough to make him want to wipe the young man's sneer off his face with his fist. Not for the first time; in fact all the time, he wondered how a straight arrow like Luke Harper had fathered a brat like Jesse Harper. Made no sense. Maybe if he asked his friend, he'd get a second surprise to add to Hank Boothroyd's stunning revelation.

Jesse Harper crooned, 'Why, I didn't lay a finger on Lil, Marshal.'

Jackson snorted.

Harper put his hand on an imaginary Bible. 'Honest truth, so help me God.'

'Don't swear falsely,' Saul Jackson bellowed. 'Hell, Jesse. You've become a viper breed!'

Harper's sneer deepened.

Jackson's urge to plant his fist in Harper's face became almost irresistible. He warned, 'Don't buck me, Jesse. I'm not in a mood for joshing.'

'I hate to do this, but . . . well, you leave me no choice, Marshal.' He threw open the bedroom door. 'Good folk. Come on out here and talk to the Marshal, will you?'

The Broken Wheel ranny was first to appear, dishevelled and pulling up his trousers. 'What's all the damn hullabaloo Jesse?' he groused. 'Can't a man have a little fun in this burg without bein' interrupted?'

Harper said, 'You tell the marshal where I've been, Danny.'

Danny was the picture of innocence. 'Why, right here, Jesse. With Conchita and me.'

Now the Mexican whore came to the door, not bothering to get dressed, and confirmed, 'That's right, Marshal.' She laughed, lewdly. 'Some folk 'round here might frown on three in a bed. But any time you wanna try eet, Marshal. . .'

Jesse Harper and the Broken Wheel ranny leaned on each other sniggering. Harper said, 'Shame on you, Conchita. Mr Jackson is a happily married man.'

Conchita shrugged. 'Most of my customers are

happeely marreed men, fellas.'

The sniggering duo burst into outright guffawing. When he brought his laughter under control, Jesse said, 'Tell the Marshal how long we've been bedmates.'

'Why, an hour. Maybe more, Marshal,' said the ranny.

Conchita backed him up.

Jesse Harper said, 'I guess that's the end of that, Marshal Jackson. Nice talkin' to you.'

'This is not the end of it, Jesse,' the Oakville lawman said, stonily. 'You beat up on Lil Scannell – likely killed her.' His face set in ice. 'Murder in this town earns a rope.'

'Even if I did kill that bitch,' Harper flared, 'you think a Harper would be hanged in this town?'

The rancher's son had stated a fact. Oakville was a Harper town, always had been. In the good days the needs of the Broken Wheel had lined a lot of citizens' pockets, and they were hopeful that soon it would again.

'Get out of here, Marshal,' Jesse scoffed. Then, socially, he said, 'Tell Lil I'll drop by and see her at the infirmary, won't you?' He put an arm around Conchita's waist and pulled her against him. 'Later.'

Saul Jackson said with feeling, 'Maybe I should just have let that fella kill you earlier, Jesse. I reckon it would be a relief to your pa and you if I had.'

'Don't push your luck, old man,' Harper growled. 'I might just forget that you're my Pa's friend!'

On his way back to the law office, Jackson dropped by the infirmary.

'Lil's in a bad way, Saul,' Doc Flatley told him with feeling. It was no secret in town that since his wife had died a couple of years before, Wes Flatley had, on occasion, enjoyed Lil Scannell's company.

Jackson looked down on the bruised, misused and unconscious saloon dove and said, 'No woman, even a saloon whore, deserves what Jesse Harper gave you, Lil.' He asked Flatley, 'Will she pull through, Wes?'

Flatley tugged at his chest-long beard. 'Hard to say, Saul. I'll do my darnedest, but . . .' He shrugged and settled watery blue eyes on the marshal. 'Are you fixing on hauling Jesse Harper in?'

'Says he didn't lay a finger on her, Doc.' Jackson sighed wearily. 'And there's nothing I can do about it, I reckon.'

He explained Jesse Harper's crafty planning to Flatley, and concluded, 'A half-baked attorney would have him out of jail in seconds flat. And John Benjamin isn't a half-baked attorney, Wes.'

The marshal's weary resignation deepened.

'I guess Jesse Harper will ride out this storm like he's ridden out all the others in recent times.'

'What's happened to that boy?' Flatley pondered. 'He's gone hellishly bad.'

'It happens sometimes,' said Jackson. 'A man turns sour, and no-one can do a thing about it.'

The medico stated what most people in town reckoned was Jesse Harper's turning point.

'I figure he never got over Willie Brady wiping his eye with Lucy Webster, holler as he might that it didn't matter any.'

Jackson agreed.

Flatley opined, 'I figure Lucy had rocks in her head to take Willie Brady over Jesse Harper . . .'

That was not Saul Jackson's point of view.

'Being mistress of the Broken Wheel sure is a long way off being a ranch hand's wife, as she'll be if she ties the knot with Willie Brady.'

Jackson leaped to Willie's defence.

'There isn't anything wrong with Willie, Wes, other than a little poverty. But he's an honest, God-fearing man who, in my opinion, will make Lucy Webster a fine husband, if she has the good sense to grab him. I reckon that sooner rather than later, he'll have that freighting business he's been hankering to start, up and running. And I figure soon after that, Lucy Webster will be one of Oakville's luckiest and finest ladies.'

Doc Flatley chuckled. 'You always saw Willie as your boy, didn't you, Saul?'

'I reckon so,' the lawman admitted.

'You and Martha regret letting Willie go to Luke Harper, don't you?'

'That's for sure, Wes. But Luke took Willie Brady in as his own, and Willie's been really fortunate in having a man of Luke Harper's calibre to provide for his needs.'

'You know, Saul,' Wes Flatley murmured, 'it's funny that Harper never gave Willie the start-up cash he needs for that freighting business, wouldn't you say?'

Jackson, unable to answer Flatley's question without breaking a confidence and revealing Luke Harper's precarious financial position, said, 'It isn't rightly any of our business, Wes.'

Before Jackson left the infirmary Flatley's final conclusion was, 'I reckon Willie will never get enough capital together to make his dream come true. Unless he robs the damn bank!'

'That's not Willie's style,' Jackson confidently assured the medico.

But Flatley replied, sagely, 'Don't know, Saul. Desperate men do desperate deeds. And right now, with Lucy Webster giving Willie the cold shoulder, he might just be desperate enough to try anything.'

'Not Willie Brady,' Marshal Jackson avowed.

FOUR

Right at that moment, Willie Brady was on the receiving end of Lucy Webster's tongue-lashing. 'You're not ever going to get the kind of money you need from punching cows at the Broken Wheel, Willie.'

Willie had, against his better judgement, knowing from past ruckuses that Lucy was a slow-cooling woman, dropped by the Webster house to reason with her. It was a bad idea, he was learning.

'I'll talk to my brother, Charlie. Ask him to help out.'

'That's a crazy notion,' Willie groaned. 'Why would Charlie want to finance 'nother freighter in opposition to him. That don't make no sense, Lucy.'

'Well, how about you coming to work for Charlie. In time you two could work out a partnership deal. Charlie isn't really a freighter anyway. He just had to take over when Pa was bushwhacked ten years ago. He sees himself rivalling Andrew Benton as a banker one day soon.'

Willie Brady was shaking his head, fit to come off.

Lucy pleaded, 'Think about it, Willie. Maybe when the time comes, Charlie will just sell up. You'd have your own freight company then.'

'Lords, Lucy, I'm twenty-six years old—'

'That's nothing,' Lucy interjected. 'Charlie was twenty-eight when he took over running the freight line.'

'Twenty-eight!' Willie yelped. 'Why, I aim to have Brady Freight haulin' long before that.' He rolled his eyes. 'Twenty-eight. Heck!'

'How?' Lucy stated bluntly. 'You haven't got the money to start, Willie. And you never will have if you keep working for the Broken Wheel for little more than a bunk and grub!'

'I'll get the money,' Willie vowed. 'Don't 'xactly know how yet. But I'm thinkin' hard, Lucy honey.'

Lucy said, primly, 'Willie Brady. You let me ask Charlie for help, because like I told you, I don't aim to gather dust on the shelf.'

Angered by Lucy Webster's starchy ultimatum, Willie flung back, 'I wouldn't ask your brother for the time of day!'

'Then,' Lucy said, firmly closing the door, 'you go and find a girl who's willing to believe in your silly dreams, Willie Brady!'

His anger turning to rage, Willie took several paces back from the house and hollered, 'You just wait and see, Lucy. I'll have the shekels I need in no time at all.'

He vaulted into the saddle and galloped out of the Websters' yard, wheeling left to hit the trail for the Broken Wheel ranch. He had a plan; one he had tried his best not to implement, but he was left with little choice now that Lucy had stated her case for the second time in less than an hour. If he did not get that damn freight company up and running pronto, he'd lose her, most likely to that fop Ashley Bryant.

The financier would like nothing better than having Oakville's most beautiful woman hanging on his arm at the fancy bashes he threw at that mansion of his outside of town. In better times, Lucy Webster would not glance Ashley Bryant's way. But these were not better times. Lucy had a hankering for marriage, and he had better do something about it – fast! In the West, an old maid was something a family hoped they would never have to admit to, (having an outlaw in the family was preferable) and it was a status no woman wanted to claim. So, if he did not buck up his ideas, Lucy would jump off that shelf she was always talking about sitting on, right into Ashley Bryant's arms!

He rode to the Broken Wheel as if the devil's prong was poking his rear end, and did not draw rein until he did so in front of the ranch house.

Luke Harper, observing Willie Brady's helter-skelter arrival, had hurried from the house, fearing Willie was the bearer of bad tidings.

'Something happen to Jesse in town, Willie?' he asked, charging down the steps from the house.

'Jesse? No, sir.'

'Then what the dev—?'

Willie cut off his outburst. 'We gotta talk, Mr Harper. Urgent like.'

'Talk? What about?'

'Well, put bluntly,' said Willie, 'I need a bundle o' dollars. And I need 'em quick.'

The rancher leaned closer to sniff Willie's breath. 'You ain't been drinking.' He looked to the orb in the sky. 'So, I reckon you've taken too much sun on the head, Willie.' He shoved him towards the bunkhouse. 'You go lie down for a spell, son.'

Brady resisted the rancher's shove. 'Will you just listen to what I've got to say, Mr Harper?'

Harper glanced back to the house, where he had been working on the ranch's books; they made for gloomy reading.

'Can't it wait? I'm real busy right now, Willie.'

'No, sir,' Willie stated bluntly.

The rancher shook his head. 'I don't know what's got you so fired up. Ain't like you, Willie.'

'There's good reason,' he assured the rancher.

'Well . . .' The rancher strode towards the house. 'This parleying will have to be short. Like I said . . .'

'Yes, sir. What I have to say will take no time at all.'

A minute later, Willie Brady true to his word, Luke Harper stood in the centre of his parlour, agape. 'Did you say a thousand dollars, Willie?'

'Yes, sir. A thousand is what I reckon I'll need to buy a wagon and team and feed, and . . ..'

The rancher held up his hand to stall Willie. What he had to tell the young man was painful to him, because Willie Brady ranked high in the qualities he'd expect of a man whom he'd consider worthy to have as a friend; qualities he wished his son Jesse had, in even half the measure that Willie Brady displayed.

'I can't help you, Willie.'

'Huh?'

Harper was keenly aware that Willie was knocked back by his refusal. It added to his grief that he was not able to explain to Brady the acuteness of his indebtedness to the Oakville bank; a debt compounded even more by his additional borrowings from Ashley Bryant.

Recovering from the shock of his refusal, Willie

Brady spat, 'Won't, you mean?'

'No, son. Can't,' the rancher restated.

Willie looked around the expensively furnished room and the opulent grandeur of the house overall. When his eyes returned to Luke Harper's, they had, for the first time in the rancher's recollection, a raw bitterness.

'Real sorry I wasted your time, Mr Harper,' Willie grated. 'I guess I'll get on with my chores now.'

In the seconds it took for the front door to angrily slam shut, Harper died a thousand deaths. He wanted to go after Willie and explain his precarious financial circumstances to him. But if he did that he'd be taking a chance on showing his hand; a hand he'd played very close to his chest for over a year now. In country where jackals were quick to gather when a man went down, it would be the end of the Broken Wheel if folk thought it was not as robust an enterprise as it appeared to be.

Harper was certain of two things. Andrew Benton, the president of the Oakville bank, would cut him all the slack he could, though he knew there would come a time when Benton would have to rein him in. But Ashley Bryant, given half a chance, would tighten the noose around his neck to make a profit, or grab the Broken Wheel for himself. He had heard from

Benton, that Bryant was eyeing the Broken Wheel as a possible wedding-present for Lucy Webster. The bank president's news had come as a shock to the rancher. He had always figured on Lucy Webster and Willie Brady tying the knot, though for a spell it had looked like Lucy would become a Harper, and that would have been OK too. In fact he regretted Jesse's rejection by Lucy, and figured that that was the turn in the trail which had sent his son off seeking the kind of comforts the Happy Lizard could provide, all of them no good. Of all the twists that life could cruelly throw up, Harper reckoned that Lucy Webster becoming Mrs Ashley Bryant was the one that would stick in his craw the most.

Even more so than seeing Bryant as the lord and master of the Broken Wheel.

The thunder of hoofs brought Luke Harper to the sitting-room window, just in time to see Willie Brady flash past. His glance Harper's way was keenly unfriendly. Brady's rebellious mood was new to the rancher, and he was seeing a Willie Brady that he'd never seen before.

Willie wheeled at the exit from the ranch yard on to the trail to town, urging even more effort from his tired mount.

Harper murmured, 'Don't do anything stupid, Willie.'

FIVE

Hank Boothroyd said, 'You know, Marshal. Sooner or later you're going to have to kill that Harper *hombre*. He's trouble that will get bigger the more you indulge him.'

'You're not telling me anything I don't already know, Boothroyd,' Saul Jackson said. 'The thing is, if I kill Jesse Harper, I'll also kill the oldest and dearest friend I have in these parts.' Jackson shook his head in wonder. 'I've racked my brains trying to figure out how a man like Luke Harper could have had the kind of cur offspring that he has in Jesse.'

Hank Boothroyd's knowing glance went Jackson's way.

'Yeah,' the marshal said sourly, 'I've thought of that possibility.'

Boothroyd hauled his lanky frame out of the chair he was seated on. 'I'll be seeing you,

Marshal,' he drawled. 'You be sure to keep that secret I told you under your hat.' His tone chilled. 'Because if it gets out, you won't have a head to put a hat on.'

Jackson reacted angrily. 'I told you, Boothroyd. I react badly to threats.'

Boothroyd left a fuming marshal in his wake, straining at the leash to go after his departed visitor to haul him back to jail for threatening a peace officer. But the cat's squabble that that would make would have people asking all sorts of questions; questions he did not want asked for Willie Brady's sake.

When his anger calmed, Jackson grinned ruefully.

'How sure you are, old-timer, that you could haul Boothroyd back here.' He caught sight of his face in a fly-spotted shaving mirror, a relic from Oakville's more hectic times, when he had spent a whole passel of nights sleeping in his own jail. He told his image in the mirror, 'You're not even half fast enough to go up against Hank Boothroyd, you old fool.'

Willie Brady rode like a madman, disregarding the dangers and pitfalls of the trail back to town at his peril. To reach town as fast as he could, he had taken a little-used trail that flung up many hairy moments before he completed his journey.

He drew rein in front of the Happy Lizard saloon, leapt from his saddle and stormed up the steps to crash through the batwings, not breaking his angry stride until he was bellied-up to the bar.

'Whiskey!' he ordered.

'Whiskey, Willie?' the roly-poly barkeep checked.

'You got wax in your ears, Bob?' Willie grated.

'But you ain't a whiskey-drinkin' man, Willie,' Bob Lynch said. 'A man's gotta get used to strong liquor slowly, and over time, too. Otherwise it'll send your senses skitterin'.'

Willie Brady hammered his fist on the bartop.

'Bob Lynch,' he growled. 'If I'd wanted a lecture on the evils of hard liquor, I'd have dropped in on the Reverend Sweeney.' He took up a no-nonsense stand. 'Now, do you pour, or do I go and git it for m'self?'

'What tick's got under Willie's hide?' was the question being whispered around the saloon.

'I'm pourin' fast as I can,' Lynch griped, as Willie threatened to vault the bar, and he repeated, 'I still think it's loco for a beer-drinker to slug whiskey right off without tastin' for a spell first, Willie.'

Willie flung his money on the bartop and grabbed the bottle from the barkeep.

'You're goin' to—'

'I aim to,' Willie interjected, surlily cutting off the barkeep's agape question.

Willie Brady strode across the saloon to the drunks' table, as the table in the darkest corner of the saloon was called by the saloon's regular imbibers. He poured three quick shots and downed them quicker still, his face sour as the rot-gut hit the pit of his belly, churned, and threatened to curl back up.

Bob Lynch nodded to an old-timer who knew how much Willie Brady meant to Saul Jackson. The old-timer left the saloon and hurried to the law-office, arriving out of breath.

'Easy, Ned,' Saul Jackson advised, and helped the old-timer to a chair. He took a bottle of rye from the desk drawer and poured a slug into a tin cup. 'Get that down you.'

Ned Harvey savoured the smooth-as-silk liquor, and when finished looked longingly in to the empty cup. Smiling, Jackson poured another shot.

'Now, Ned. Why the head of steam?'

'It's Willie Brady—'

Jackson pounced. 'Willie. What about him?'

'Gettin' all liquored up in the Happy Lizard.'

'Willie?' the marshal questioned in disbelief. 'Getting liquored up?'

'Skunk drunk,' Ned Harvey confirmed. 'Never seen a man guzzle whiskey as fast afore.'

The lawman's disbelief went up another notch. 'Whiskey?' he yelped.

'Must be half-way down the bottle by now, I reckon, Marshal,' said the old-timer.

Saul Jackson was stunned by the news. Willie Brady was an easy drinking fella; a beer, maybe two at most. Shaking himself free of his inertia, the marshal grabbed his hat from the hat-rack behind his desk, rammed the Stetson on his head and strode purposefully out of the door, swinging right for the Happy Lizard.

Ned Harvey, not being a man to look a gift horse in the mouth, reached for the bottle of silken Kentucky rye and filled his tin cup to overflowing. He lounged on the couch on which the marshal took his siesta and sipped rye, holding each drop on his tongue until the last smidgen of taste had been savoured, before letting the smooth liquor slide down his throat.

'It's an ill-wind . . .' he cackled.

The Happy Lizard batwings strained on their hinges as Saul Jackson came through them with the force of an angry bull, his grey eyes searching the murky saloon. The barkeep nodded in the direction of the drunks' table, where Willie Brady was swaying in his chair, only enough rot-gut left to colour the bottom of the bottle. Jackson grabbed the bottle and slung it aside. It smashed against the far wall. Willie reacted angrily.

'What the hell did ya do that for, Marshal?' He glowered.

'You're coming with me, Willie,' Jackson commanded.

Brady shrugged off the lawman's hold. 'I ain't goin' no place 'til I'm good and reshy,' he slurred.

Jackson was resolute. 'You're leaving with me right now, Willie!'

'Seems to me, Marshal,' Jackson swung around to face a sneering Jesse Harper leaning on the batwings, 'that Willie isn't breaking any laws.'

'Stay out of it, Jesse,' Jackson ordered.

'Don't know if I can, Marshal,' the rancher's son drawled lazily. 'Seems to me that a citizen's, and a friend's rights,' he crossed the saloon to place a comradely arm about Willie Brady's shoulders, 'are being shucked aside.'

'Yeah. Jeshee's right, Marshal Jackshon,' Willie mumbled drunkenly.

Uncompromisingly, Saul Jackson said, 'You're drunk, Willie. Drunkenness is against town law.'

Jesse Harper scoffed. 'You're not going to have a jail big enough, if you go and lock up every drunk, Jackson. Willie is only having a good time. No law against having a good time, that I know of.'

A couple of town dregs, who were enjoying the benefits of Jesse Harper's largesse during his stay in town, backed their benefactor.

Saul Jackson stood firm.

'Willie is going to jail for his own good. He's had his first lick of whiskey. It's scattered his senses.'

'I ain't goin' t' no damn jail, and that's final, Marshha . . . al!'

Jesse Harper, maliciously in Jackson's opinion, stoked Willie Brady's drunken rebellion. 'I'm with you on this, Willie, old friend.'

Jackson again grabbed Willie's arm to escort him out of the saloon. Brady pushed him away. His hand dived for his gun, thumb fumbling with the hammer. The marshal, angered by Willie's attempt at gunplay, kicked the pistol from his grasp and slapped him hard across the face. Willie spun backwards over the drunks' table. When he got up, nursing his right cheek, an evil fire that Saul Jackson never thought he'd see in the young man's eyes blazed fiercely. It pained him to the core of his heart to have to witness the hatred contorting Willie Brady's sobering features.

'No call for what you just done, Marshal,' he said, in a spite-laden tone.

'You left me with no choice, Willie. You drew iron. Count yourself lucky that the price you paid for your foolishness wasn't much higher.'

Jesse Harper sneered. 'Willie was no threat, Marshal. You hit him 'cause you were riled by his independent mood.'

'I figure Jesse is callin' it right,' one of the men whom the rancher's son had been plying with free liquor piped up.

'Mind your own damn business, Brent!' Jackson flung back.

Johnny Brent swaggered forward aggressively. 'I got a right to an opinion, too, Jackson,' he spat. 'You sayin' I ain't?'

Jackson snapped, 'I'm saying keep your mouth shut or feel my fist in it!'

Brent pulled himself up to his full height of six foot three inches. 'I don't take kindly to what you just said, Marshal.'

Jackson flung back, 'And I don't give a damn, Brent!'

The argument between the marshal and Willie Brady fitted in glovelike with a plan that had been coming together in Jesse Harper's mind since he had overheard a snippet of conversation on a visit to the Silver Eagle hotel a couple of minutes before, which had set in motion his plan to quit Oakville for ever. And now, if he was really clever, he could make his plan risk free.

He let his eyes drift Johnny Brent's way, carrying the message to back off. Brent, used to trouble-stirring for one faction or another, instantly and correctly read his benefactor's intentions. Right away, he dropped his challenge to Saul Jackson.

'I ain't looking for no trouble with the law, Marshal,' said Brent, a snake-oil smile flourishing on his mean lips.

'Wise move,' Jackson said.

Jesse Harper assumed the role of peacemaker.

'Marshal. What do you say to me fixing Willie up with a room here at the Happy Lizard? When he sleeps off his binge, I'll put him on his horse and point him towards the Broken Wheel.'

It was a compromise that was hard to argue against without outraging Willie Brady further, and suffering entirely the loss of the young man's friendship; something that Jackson was loath to do.

'I guess,' the lawman reluctantly conceded, preferring to take Willie Brady under his wing than let him hang around the Happy Lizard, which was the focal point for most of Oakville's trouble. He worried too about Jesse Harper's influence over the youngster. The rancher's son had, in the months since he went bad, become Oakville's prime corrupter.

'That's settled then,' said Harper. 'Bob . . .'

'Yeah,' the barkeep answered.

'Put clean sheets on a bed for my friend, Willie.' He laughed slyly. 'And make sure that there isn't one of the Happy Lizard's comely doves in it, huh?'

The sleazy laughter that rang around the

saloon raised Saul Jackson's hackles to full stretch. He warned Harper, 'I'm making you personally responsible for Willie's safe delivery, Jesse.'

'There's no harm going to come to him,' the rancher's son assured the lawman. ' 'Cept maybe if Conchita or one of the Happy Lizard's other beauties takes a shine to Willie and shows him some pleasurable tricks.'

'No women – no liquor!' ordered Jackson.

'Why, Marshal Jackson,' Jesse Harper chuckled, 'you planning on filling heaven?'

Harper and his cohort's mocking laughter licked Jackson's heels as he stormed out of the saloon. He beelined for the law-office, figuring on a shot of rye to cool his temper. Nearing the office he heard raucous singing and much giggling. He flung open the door. On seeing the empty rye-bottle rolling across the floor to meet him, his suspicions were confirmed.

Ned Harvey lay sprawled on the couch like a drunken Roman emperor. He waved gaily at Jackson, before he rolled on to the floor, snoring loudly before he reached it. Jackson picked up the empty rye-bottle and sighed.

'Not having the best of days, huh, Marshal?'

The lawman swung around to slam the door shut on Hank Boothroyd's smirking face. He hauled the old-timer to a cell to sleep off his spree. He came back into the office from the jail, flung himself into the Douglas chair behind his desk and growled, 'No, Mr Boothroyd. I'm not having a good day.' His frown deepened. 'And you know what, I've got a feeling that I've only seen the tip of the iceberg yet!'

SIX

The evening lengthened into night, and still Saul Jackson's humour had not sweetened any. He had made trip after trip to the law-office door to look the way of the Happy Lizard for any sign of brewing trouble. The noise from the saloon had steadily grown in raucousness, as was the norm, as men were drawn to music and the bright lights after a day's drudgery. The lilting voice of the saloon's resident songstress, an Irish girl by the name of Maud Hanlon, spilled pleasantly out of the saloon, accompanied by Benny Rodman's easy-on-the-ear ivory-tinkling. Maud's ditty was a humorous Irish song about a farmer and a goat, both of whom had a stubborn streak, with neither prepared to back off. Despite his gloom, Jackson smiled. The song had many parallels in the West, where stubbornness often led to the kind of trouble the Irish farmer was having with his goat – or worse.

'A touch edgy, aren't you, Marshal?' Hank Boothroyd drifted out of the shadows. The man moved with the stealth of a cat. Jackson reckoned that he could step on eggs and not crack them. Perceptively homing in on the marshal's thoughts, he said, 'Willie was still sleeping the last time I checked. Been keeping an eye on him, Marshal. Figured you wouldn't be very welcome in the Happy Lizard right now.'

Jackson was grateful. 'Obliged, Mr Boothroyd.'

'I'd prefer if you called me Hank.'

'Wouldn't be fitting,' the lawman said. 'We walk paths on different sides of this badge I'm toting. Best we keep our relationship and conduct our business with that fact in mind.'

Hank Boothroyd grinned. 'You've got a lot of starch in you, Marshal.'

'Have you spoken to Willie Brady yet?'

'Isn't the right time,' the gunfighter said.

Intrigued, Jackson asked, 'What do you think he'll say when you tell him your news?'

Boothroyd hunched his shoulders. 'Don't believe in crossing bridges before I come to them, Marshal Jackson. In my line of work, the future is not worth pondering about.'

Jackson said, 'Makes sense. Can't but think, though, that Willie will be a mighty surprised fella when you do get round to telling him.'

Boothroyd said, 'Maybe mad as hell, too.'

Maud Hanlon's song had ended to rousing applause. A chorus of voices requested various songs from Maud's extensive repertoire. She obliged with a song about a cowboy who sat on a cactus and was never the same again. When the final rousing chorus of that song finished, Willie Brady's voice rose above everyone else's to request the kind of song which, if sung, would have the town's Puritan League marching on the morrow.

'Seems Willie has woken up. Best look in on him,' said Boothroyd.

Jackson pulled him back. 'I'll go.'

'Not sure if that's a good idea, Marshal,' the gunfighter opined. 'Figure that a wart on a fella's ladies' delight might be more welcome than you'll be in the Happy Lizard right now.'

'I'm the damn marshal!' Jackson stubbornly declared. 'In this burg, I go where I please, mister.'

The Oakville badge-toter strode away.

Hank Boothroyd murmured, 'Might be marching to your own funeral, Marshal.'

When Jackson pushed through the Happy Lizard bat-wings, a hush as deep as that found inside a coffin stilled the saloon's rowdy antics. Willie Brady was at the bar looking the worse for wear, and intent on making himself even more reprehensible-looking if the half-finished bottle of rot-gut in front of him was his.

As Jackson strode up to Willie, Jesse Harper and his cronies moved in behind him to cut off his retreat. The mood in the bar changed from grudging to outright menacing. Willie Brady turned from the bar, and it pained the marshal to observe his drunken stupor. He looked like any other bottle-chasing bum in the Happy Lizard.

'Time to go home, Willie,' said Jackson.

'Dang it, Marshal.' Liquor ran down Willie Brady's chin. 'How many times do I have to tell you that I'm able to look out for m'self?'

Johnny Brent, now constantly at Jesse Harper's side, sucking up to him, stepped forward.

'You seem intent on throwin' a wet blanket over men's pleasure, Jackson.' His eyes swept the saloon's patrons. 'And I reckon folk are sick and tired of your interferin'.'

Saul Jackson was not a cowardly man, but he was no fool either. The mood in the bar was sliding towards anarchy, and it would not take a great deal of provocation to bring its simmering to the boil. He was headed into an argument he could not win. But he knew that if he backed down, he would never win again.

Brent crowded the marshal.

'I reckon you should shove off now, Marshal.'

Jackson said stonily, 'I'll leave when I'm good and ready, Brent. Not before!'

Brent, enjoying the backing of his cronies and a good number of the other imbibers, kept pushing. 'Leave or be carried, Jackson,' he growled. 'The choice is yours.'

Now the mood changed again. Except for Jesse Harper and the men with him, the other drinkers began to slink away, not wanting anything to do with a killing; and the killing of a lawman to boot. Brent's stance and mood changed. Saul Jackson was facing a gunfight. Brent was fast, and the lawman wasn't at all sure that he could match him. Support came from Willie Brady, who had been sobered by the threat to Jackson's well-being.

'Ain't no call for no killin', Johnny,' said Willie.

Brent looked with hostile contempt at Willie Brady. 'Dive back into your bottle, Brady,' he snorted. Willie, incensed by Brent's scoffing attitude shoved Jackson aside, settling his awry gunbelt on his narrow hips.

'Settle down, Willie,' Jackson urged. 'I'll deal with this cur.'

Brent sniggered: 'I'll drop you 'fore you reach iron, old man,' he promised. 'Brady, too.'

'If you want a fight . . .' All eyes went to Hank

Boothroyd standing in the bat wings. 'Fight me, you rat's ass!'

Brent paled, recognizing in Hank Boothroyd the angel of death. But with his pride goaded he chanced his luck and drew. Boothroyd's Colt .45 might have been in his hand all the time, it appeared in it so fast. It bucked. Brent was lifted clear off his feet and crashed against the bar, his back arcing. The snap of his spine rang out as clear as a Sunday church-bell over the prairie, but it mattered none to Johnny Brent.

He was already dead.

Jackson was furious. He knew that a drawn gun invited other guns.

'Anyone hand you an invite to this shindig?' he blasted the gunfighter.

Stonily, Boothroyd answered, 'You're forgetting my special interest in the proceedings, Marshal.'

'What special interest, mister?' Jesse Harper angrily quizzed the gunslinger.

'None of your damn business!' the gunfighter flung back. His face frosted over. 'Unless . . .' He slid the .45 back into its holster and faced Harper squarely.

Jesse Harper's eyes widened. Quickly he assured Boothroyd, 'I haven't got a quarrel with you, sir.'

Wearily, Jackson took Willie Brady's arm. 'Come on, Willie. You can bunk down at my house tonight.'

'I'm real sorry, Marshal Jackson,' Willie apologized.

Jackson smiled. 'Forget it, Willie. Most men fall off their pedestal sooner or later.'

On his way out of the saloon, Willie paused to thank Hank Boothroyd. 'I guess you saved my hide, Mr . . .?'

'Boothroyd. Hank Boothroyd.'

Willie Brady's were not the only wide-open eyes in the Happy Lizard. Awestruck, Willie asked, 'The gunfighter? That Hank Boothroyd?'

'Same,' Boothroyd confirmed.

'Jeez!'

'You get a good night's sleep, son,' Boothroyd said, his voice soft and his eyes warm.

'Can you believe that?' Willie kept asking Saul Jackson as they walked the short distance to the marshal's house. 'Hank Boothroyd. Right here in Oakville, too. Gosh!'

'Got a guest needing bed and board, Martha,' Jackson called out as he entered the house.

Martha Jackson came from the kitchen, rubbing flour from her hands on a gingham apron. Her eyes lit with the fire of welcome on seeing Willie Brady with her husband. Then, taking in Willie's shoddy appearance, concern clouded them.

'Sorry I look like somethin's the cat dragged in, Mrs Jackson,' Willie mumbled. 'I've acted real stupid, ma'am.'

Martha Jackson's glance went to her husband.

He said, 'It's a long story not worth the telling, Martha.'

As always, Martha Jackson took her man's word. She had never had reason to think that he had anything but her welfare at heart, and she was satisfied to be mollycoddled.

'I've got fresh bread,' she enthused. 'Broth and cheese, too. Then apple pie, of course.'

Willie complimented, 'Shucks, Mrs Jackson, ma'am. You bake the best apple pie in the whole darn West.'

A flush of pleasure took some of the worry-laden years off Martha Jackson's face. 'Why, Willie Brady. You were surely born with a silver tongue!' Preening herself, she hurried off to the kitchen.

Jackson said, 'Before you get a bite of that apple pie, young man, you'll bathe. You'll find hot water a-plenty in the kitchen and a tub out back. Git!'

Willie clicked his heels and saluted. 'Yes, sir!'

Out back, oil-lamp in hand, Willie Brady was unaware of Hank Boothroyd's watching and admiring eyes on him.

SEVEN

Henry Jasper, the Pinkerton detective who was to convey Ashley Bryant's money back east, sat in the financier's office with a shotgun across his lap. The safe held the cash that the Pinkerton agency had been employed by Bryant to protect and deliver.

The night had passed without incident, and it was waning when he stood up to stretch. He was relieved that the night was almost over, with dawn showing its first streaks in the black sky. He had spent the night sitting in the dark, not lighting a lamp lest it should attract the kind of attention that he wanted to avoid. The plan was for him to slip quietly out of town at first light. He had been booked into the Silver Eagle hotel for two more nights, and the story was that he was confined to his room with a chill. It was a good plan. There was another Pinkerton man in the hotel room who, with drawn blinds, was close enough in appearance to pass as him. He had intentionally kept his presence around town to a minimum since he had arrived on the stage, while his accomplice had drifted into town during the night to take his place in the hotel room. It was a ploy that had been successfully used by the Pinkerton detective agency on more than one occasion. The plan was for the second Pinkerton detective to leave town in a couple of days when he would be joined outside town by three more men, in case of trouble. By then Jasper would be long gone, and well on his way out of danger with Ashley Bryant's money. As an added precaution, he alone would decide on his route back East.

It was a foolproof plan.

Of course, the West being the lawless territory that it was, things did not always go according to plan. Detective Henry Jasper knew this, but had not expected the surprise in store as he drank a cup of coffee before setting off on his journey.

'Jasper,' the voice was notched in a low whisper, but did not cause the detective any unease. 'Open up, I forgot the key to this door isn't on my chain.'

Unconcerned, the Pinkerton agent strode to the side door that opened on to the alley at the side of the office to let Ashley Bryant in. It was not in the plan for him to come calling, but Henry

Jasper reckoned that a man parting with the bounty that he was, would want to check that everything was in order.

When he opened the door, a shape sprang from the shadows with the swiftness of a starving mountain cat. A narrow, wicked blade flashed. It was plunged into Jasper's windpipe. He stumbled back into the office, clutching at the dagger, blood pouring down his shirtfront. As he sank to the floor, the Pinkerton man saw and recognized his killer. He was one of the men whom he had seen in the saloon fracas at the Happy Lizard the previous day. Jasper tried to call out, but the man bent down and drove the dagger deeper into his windpipe. The blade came out the back of his neck and pinned him to the floor.

The murderer casually searched Jasper's pockets for the key to the safe. Finding it, he opened the safe and removed the bulging saddle-bags inside. He opened them to check their contents, and knew that whatever dreams and ambitions he had, they were now sure to come to pass.

All he had to do was bide his time. He had already planned carefully.

Saul Jackson was pouring the dish of shaving water over his head when Willie Brady came round the side of the house, out of breath.

'You're up and about early, Willie,' the marshal observed.

'Sure am.'

'Any particular reason?'

'I saw someone raiding your hen-house. I gave chase, but he had a head start and could run like the damn wind, too. Didn't get his pilferin' hands on any chickens though. Lucky I woke up when I did.'

'I guess it was.' Jackson laughed. 'Imagine that, Willie. A damn chicken-rustler.'

They laughed heartily at the idea.

Willie said, 'All we gotta do is find a gent with chicken-shit on his boots, I reckon.'

Their laughter soared.

'Reckon I should ask that Pinkerton detective to help out, Willie?'

They were still laughing when they reached the kitchen, and periodically during breakfast their bout of jollity erupted again. The hammering on the front door put an end to their latest outburst of mirth.

'Who can that be this early?' Martha Jackson speculated.

'Unless you can see through the door, you'll have to open it to find out, Martha,' said Jackson mischievously.

'Well, knock me down with a feather,' said Martha Jackson. 'But aren't you the smart one,

Saul Jackson. And just a spit from cockcrow too.'

As a fist thundered on the door again, Willie Brady said, 'Maybe one of the chickens got out and is tryin' to get back in.'

Jackson shook with laughter.

A moment later his laughter was curtailed, when Ashley Bryant appeared in the kitchen looking paler than a corpse in the back room of the funeral parlour. As he staggered against the kitchen door, Willie grabbed him.

'Best sit, Bryant,' Jackson advised, shoving a chair under the financier. 'Beforc you fall down.' Already buckling on his gunbelt, because it looked like he was going on duty right then, the marshal asked, 'What's happened?'

Ashley Bryant mumbled, 'I've been robbed, Marshal.' His next statement made robbery seem tame. 'And Henry Jasper, the Pinkerton detective, has been murdered!'

EIGHT

There was more hammering on the marshal's front door, quickly followed by Martha Jackson's scream and the thud of her fainting body on the hall floor.

'What the dev . . .?' Jackson growled.

The shock that Martha had suffered was repeated a second later for Willie Brady and Saul Jackson when Henry Jasper's double entered the kitchen supporting Martha Jackson. Willie fell back, wide-eyed, as a body would on seeing a ghost.

'Put your eyes back in their sockets and pour some coffee, Willie,' Jackson ordered. 'The dead don't walk.'

Seated at the table, Martha slowly recovered her composure, as Ashley Bryant explained, 'This gent is Frank Crane.' The mortgage-lender then went on to explain the Pinkerton plan about

Crane remaining behind in his hotel, masquerading as Henry Jasper and claiming to be poorly. 'To give Jasper time to put distance between him and Oakville.'

Crane picked up the explanation. 'A couple of days later, when Jasper was clean away, I'd leave town as him.'

'Kind of risky for you, Crane,' Jackson observed.

'I was teaming up with a couple of other Pinkerton men outside of town, all sharpshooters. We figured we could handle any trouble brewing. We've used the ploy successfully many times before.'

Willie Brady said, 'Seems to me, Mr Crane, that you fellas were holding the rough end of the stick.'

Crane said, 'Like being a lawman, flying lead is all part of being a Pinkerton detective, son.'

Marshal Jackson, who had been sizing up Frank Crane, murmured, 'Crane . . . Frank Cra . . .' He snapped his fingers as his thoughts came together. 'Hawk Crane?'

The Pinkerton man smiled. 'I haven't been called Hawk for a long time, Marshal.'

Willie Brady's eyes, sparking with curiosity, flashed from Jackson to Crane. He had heard of Hawk Crane and his exploits down around the border.

'Heard you had handed in your badge,' said Jackson. 'After Mary's death . . .'

Hawk Crane's eyes clouded with a grief that, though three years old, was as keen as if his wife's murder had happened only a second ago. The circumstances of Crane's resignation from his marshal's post in a rough-and-tumble end-of-trail Texas cow town came flooding back to Jackson. The events of that awful and foul deed, related to Jackson by a trail boss who was passing through town, came to mind. Frank Crane had been trying to corral a couple of brothers who had arrived in Saddlers Springs, where he had been the badge-toter, for the rape and murder of a farmer's wife along the cattle-drive.

Crane had caged one of the Bell twins, and was hunting down his brother when the men grabbed Mary Crane coming out of the hardware store and had held her hostage. Crane had ordered his deputy to set the incarcerated twin Mikey free, on Simon Bell's demand. But, mean as spitting rattlers by nature, the Bell brothers took Mary Crane with them as insurance, promising to release her as soon as they had put a safe distance between them and Saddlers Springs, and could see no dust on their back-trail. Crane had held to his promise, but as the evening shadows lengthened, he knew that he had made the wrong decision, and had let his feelings for his wife cloud his judgement. Trusting the Bells had been the act of a fool. The next day he had found his wife of six months tied to a tree, dead and naked, evidence of her suffering in every inch of her bruised and abused body.

Hawk Crane had returned to town, buried his wife and handed in his badge. He relentlessly tracked the Bell twins, following their trail of mayhem and murder to a mining tent-town in Montana where, without qualm, he had shot them both.

For a time he had disappeared off the face of the earth, grieving for his wife, before he turned up again sporting the badge of a Pinkerton detective.

'I hate to cut across your social chit-chat, gents!' Ashley Bryant snapped. 'But while you chinwag, someone is hightailing it with my money!'

'The man's right,' said Hawk Crane.

'Can't dispute that it's so,' Jackson agreed.

'Well,' Bryant's angry glare took in both men, 'what're you going to do about it?'

'What I can't understand, is why Henry Jasper opened the office door so readily?' Crane pondered. 'Doesn't fit in with Jasper's cautious nature.'

'Guess he reckoned there musta been no danger.'

All eyes went Willie Brady's way.

Saul Jackson said, 'Makes sense to me.'

'The next question is, I figure,' Willie said, 'is why this Jasper fella thought there was no danger?'

'Makes sense, too. You got any more ideas on this, Willie?' the marshal encouraged.

Willie Brady's brow furrowed. 'Reckon so, Marshal.'

'Well, let's have them, son,' the Oakville lawman invited.

Willie took a moment to gather his thoughts, before continuing, 'Seems to me that this Jasper *hombre* opened the door 'cause he figured he knew who was a-calling.'

'It's you who should be the Pinkerton detective 'round here,' Frank Crane opined.

'You figure so, Mr Crane?' Willie puffed out his chest, and concluded, 'Yeah. I figure mebbe you're right at that, sir.'

Jackson grabbed his hat from the edge of the kitchen table and slapped the Stetson on his head, leaving unruly tufts of his uncombed grey-flecked hair sticking out from under; a clear indication of his agitated state, him being a man who was most particular about his appearance.

'Best view the scene of the crime, I guess.'

Bryant, Crane and Willie Brady trailed the marshal to the front door, where he enquired of

Brady, 'And where do you think you're headed?' stopping the young man dead in his tracks.

'I figured—'

'It's time you headed back to the Broken Wheel to earn your keep, Willie,' Jackson interjected. 'And when you get there, tell Luke Harper to come and fetch Jesse back to the ranch, before he gets himself killed by his brash behaviour.'

Frustrated by his dismissal, Willie grumbled, 'Seems to me that I'm the real detective 'round here, Marshal Jackson.'

Jackson said, 'I'm beholden to you for your clever thinking, Willie.'

Willie Brady smiled broadly. 'I figured you would be, Marshal.'

He was about to tag along when the lawman growled, 'Git, Willie!'

Willie Brady headed for the livery, grumbling, 'Shucks!'

Jackson called after him, 'And don't forget to tell your boss to come and collect his boy, Willie.'

Looking after Willie Brady, Hawk Crane remarked, thoughtfully, 'There goes a smart young feller, Marshal.' His thoughtful frown deepened. 'I reckon his drawing of the scene at Mr Bryant's office might be uncannily correct.'

Jackson chuckled. 'Willie's a bundle of surprises, sure enough.'

As Jackson took the lead to Ashley Bryant's

office, Crane murmured to himself, 'The question is. How many surprises has he got in him, Marshal?'

On entering Ashley Bryant's office, Saul Jackson's belly took a tumble on seeing the stiletto pinning Jasper to the floor. A pool of dark blood spread out from under the Pinkerton detective's head, resembling, Jackson thought, the map of Texas. Though a lawman for twenty-odd years, he had never managed to quell his queasiness at the smell of blood in his nostrils.

'Blood is fresh,' Hawk Crane observed. 'No congealing. I figure the murder isn't very old. Diplomatically, the Pinkerton man sought Jackson's opinion. 'You reckon, Marshal?'

'I'm not a trained detective. But I reckon so,' the lawman agreed.

Crane continued his reasoning, 'So the killer couldn't have got very far?'

'Reckon not,' the Oakville marshal agreed again.

'Might even be still here in...' The plod of Willie Brady's horse interrupted Crane as he rode past on Main, 'town,' the Pinkerton detective concluded.

'Ah-huh,' Jackson mumbled.

Bryant was heading for the door. 'So, let's find him!'

Crane crossed to look out of the office window

after Willie Brady. 'Of course on the other hand . . .' He left his sentence unfinished.

Ashley Bryant was annoyed. 'You're the damn detective, Crane. Which is it? Has Jasper's killer vamoosed with my money? Or is he still in town?'

Jackson backed the financier. 'Riddles might be dandy for a Pinkerton detective, Crane. But in Oakville riddles get a cantankerous reception.'

'No tracks out of town. I checked.'

Saul Jackson cursed silently. A check for fresh tracks should have been his first action.

'Except, of course, Willie Brady's right now,' said Crane.

'But there would be a thousand hoof-marks, Crane,' Bryant flung at the detective. 'Oakville's a busy town. Lots of coming and going.'

The Pinkerton detective explained, 'Fresh tracks leave a firm imprint, Mr Bryant. Old tracks get smudged. It takes time for fresh tracks to get that worn look. Besides, there was a wind blowing last night which would have obliterated previous hoof-marks.'

Ashley Bryant's questioning and accusing gaze settled on Jackson. The marshal was too busy kicking his own butt to be perturbed by the financier's hostile scrutiny. Hawk Crane had just taught him a lesson in detection skills, and that was not settling very well with him.

Bryant, a spiteful man by nature, was not

letting him off the hook. 'Why didn't you think of that, Jackson?' he blazed.

Hawk Crane jumped to the lawman's defence. 'Marshal Jackson is not a trained detective, Mr Bryant.'

Bryant, like a dog with a bone, was not letting go.

'Seems to me that you don't have to be much of a detective to figure as you've figured, Crane,' the mortgage-lender groused.

Though Jackson appreciated Crane's attempt to redeem his standing, he'd have much preferred it if, in the first place, he'd kept his trap shut until he could give him the benefit of his Pinkerton detective training in private. However, once his ire eased, Jackson reasoned that having had the responsibility for keeping Bryant's money safe from thieves, Hawk Crane had his own worries to contend with. The Pinkerton reputation would take a hard knock when news of what had happened in Oakville got out. And that hard knock would work through to Frank Crane personally.

'So, you figure Henry Jasper's murderer is still in town?' the Oakville marshal quizzed the Pinkerton agent.

Preoccupied with his last sight of Willie Brady as he disappeared round the bend at the end of Main, Hawk Crane's murmured reply could have been a yes or a no. The Pinkerton detective's thoughtful perusal of Willie had not been lost on Saul Jackson. Thoughts were piling into the marshal's head, too; thoughts he did not want to think about.

'Crane! Is the killer still in town, man?' Ashley Bryant demanded.

The Pinkerton detective turned from the window, his eyes locking with Jackson's. 'Unless he left in the last ten minutes or so, Mr Bryant.'

'Then he's right here,' Bryant enthused. 'No one has left town in the last ten minutes except that slow-wit, Willie Brady.'

'Willie is not a slow-wit, Bryant!' said Jackson, hotly. His rock-steady gaze was directed at Hawk Crane. 'Willie Brady is a fine and honest young man.'

Ashley Bryant backtracked under the marshal's fury.

'You know what I mean, Marshal Jackson.' He slunk away from the lawman's withering stare. Then, clawing back some of his fleeing courage, the financier declared, 'Well, Willie Brady doesn't amount to much, does he?'

Frank Crane wondered about the lawman's spirited defence of Willie Brady. He recalled Brady's features, but dismissed the idea that was coming to mind. Willie Brady looked nothing like Saul Jackson. Yet, gnawingly, Willie Brady's slant of jaw and eyes rang a bell.

'We have to organize a search of every house in town,' said Ashley Bryant.

Jackson said, 'We can't just go busting in doors. Folk have a right to their privacy.'

'Not when it's my hundred thousand dollars that's gone missing!' the mortgage-lender raged.

'A hundred thou . . .' Jackson was aghast. 'Haven't you ever heard of banks?'

'As yet, the banking system is a dice game, Marshal,' the financier said. 'Would you drop a sack full of money into a maze full of crooks and charlatans?'

Jackson recalled the story of Ashley Bryant's mistrust of banks and bankers, of his having lost his first savings to a crooked banker who fled overnight with every cent of his customers' savings.

Hawk Crane leapt to his employer's defence. 'The Pinkerton Agency has a fine record in money conveyance, Marshal Jackson.'

Jackson's face curled sourly. 'I guess *had* fits the bill.'

The Pinkerton man flinched. 'I'll recover Mr Bryant's money,' he promised, and tagged on, 'Henry Jasper's murderer, too.'

'Reckon you know where to look?' Jackson quizzed, sternly.

'I've got ideas,' Crane flung back.

'Make sure they're the right ideas, Crane,' the

marshal cautioned. 'Not just any old neck in a noose will do.' His gaze unflinchingly held the Pinkerton man's. 'Not in my town, it won't!'

'Damn you, Marshal,' Crane reacted angrily. 'I never hung a man on the wrong.'

Knowing Hawk Crane's reputation as a lawman, Jackson knew this to be true. His eyes said as much in apology.

As they left Bryant's office, the town undertaker leading the way with Henry Jasper's body, Jesse Harper watched the sombre procession from upstairs in the Happy Lizard.

'Come back to bed, honey,' Conchita Murales murmured sleepily. The whore held her head, grimacing, and fell back on the pillow. She was instantly asleep again.

Taking off his hat to smooth down his unkempt hair, Jackson saw Jesse Harper at the Happy Lizard's upstairs window. He wondered how a man, who apparently had just gotten out of bed, looked so street-presentable.

The smile which Jesse Harper flashed at the Oakville marshal was a foxy one.

NINE

'Walk with me,' Jackson invited Hawk Crane.

'Where are you headed?' Ashley Bryant asked anxiously, as the pair strode off towards the law-office. 'What are you planning on doing?'

'That's just what we're aiming to talk about,' Jackson answered the mortgage lender impatiently.

The marshal called a half-dozen men to him from the crowd now forming on Main, buzzing with the news of Henry Jasper's murder and Bryant's loss. The town was quickly dividing along lines of sympathy for the financier from those who had not suffered the burden of his exorbitant interest charges, and gloating from those who had. But the town was united in their attitude to the Pinkerton detective's murder. That, the general opinion was, deserved rope justice.

Assigning the responsibility of the task he had

in mind to a tall, angular-faced man called Honest Jim Brody, (an appendage earned because of his fair dealings) the men dispersed to opposite ends of town to enforce Jackson's order to stop anyone leaving until progress was made in solving the crimes.

'When do I get my money back, Jackson?' Ashley Bryant griped. 'Why don't you search every damn man and house in town?'

'A man's been murdered, Bryant!' The Oakville marshal sternly rebuked the financier. 'And in my book, solving Henry Jasper's murder comes a long way ahead of finding your dollars.'

Bryant spat back, 'Jasper was paid to do a job which he messed up on!'

Jackson's normal disdain for the greedy financier upped a notch. Hawk Crane, too, showed signs of thinning patience with the Pinkerton client.

Headed along Main, Crane said, 'I reckon I know what you want to talk about, Marshal.'

Jackson retorted sarcastically, 'Guess, you being a Pinkerton detective, you would at that.'

Though ruffled some by the lawman's scathing remark, Crane let it pass. At least until Jackson unloaded the burden that had humped his shoulders; a hump that had shaped itself as Willie Brady had ridden out of town under the detective's watching eye.

Jackson swung through the law-office door and grabbed the coffee-pot on the stove. He rinsed out the previous day's dregs, flung in a fistful of Java beans, added water from a pump out back, fired up the stove. He placed the coffee-pot on the stove, shuffled around some paperwork on his desk, finally dropped on to the creaking old Douglas chair.

'That was a whole lot of scooting about, Marshal,' the Pinkerton detective observed. 'I take it that your thoughts have been finally drawn together?'

Jackson cast a moody eye Crane's way. 'Guess so.'

The former lawman turned Pinkerton pulled up a chair. 'So, let's parley.'

Jackson used the excuse of the boiling coffee-pot to gain another couple of minutes. The fact was, he did not want to put into words the thoughts circling in his mind; they were much too bitter to want to give voice to.

Crane pinned him down.

'Are your thoughts, like mine, on Willie Brady?'

The marshal swung around, his grey eyes fiery. 'Don't push, Crane. It's the decent thing to do to let a man pick his own time to speak.'

Hawk Crane took off his hat and swept back a shock of ginger hair, an inheritance from his Irish ancestry. 'Thing is, Marshal, we don't have the kind of time you want. Brady rode out,' he consulted his pocket-watch, 'all of thirty minutes ago.'

Jackson testily returned, 'A man can't go far in thirty minutes on the kind of windless nag that Willie is on board!'

'It's been my experience, and I'm sure yours too, Marshal Jackson that a guilty man can cover a lot of miles in thirty minutes.'

'Willie Brady isn't guilty of anything,' the marshal proclaimed loyally.

Crane went to the window to look at the thunderheads gathering to the south of town. They had been a concern since they had left Ashley Bryant's office.

'Storm coming,' he informed the Oakville lawman.

'I've got eyes!'

The Pinkerton detective turned from the window to resolutely face the marshal. 'Storms wash away tracks. If Brady's our man, his sign will soon be gone.'

Jackson had to concede the legitimacy of Hawk Crane's concern. He had no personal stake in Willie Brady's welfare; his only job was to retrieve Ashley Bryant's dollars. Even apprehending Henry Jasper's murderer would come second to that task. He was a Pinkerton agent with an unhappy client, and that, if the problem was not solved quickly and satisfactorily, would mean a passel of unhappy Pinkerton clients. The Pinkerton passwords were security and safety, which they had admirably lived up to. If it were shown to be otherwise, business would vanish as quickly as water through a holed bucket.

With a leaden heart, Saul Jackson confessed, 'Willie Brady was up and about round the time Jasper was murdered.'

'Ah-huh,' was Hawk Crane's only response, leaving the marshal to tell his story in his own time.

'Coffee?'

Crane declined the lawman's hospitality.

Jackson rolled a smoke and puffed as he supped. He said, 'Willie says he was chasing a chicken-thief he'd seen in my hen-house.'

The Pinkerton detective asked, 'Believe him?'

'Sure, I do!'

Frank Crane searched Jackson's eyes.

The marshal said, limply, 'Never known Willie Brady to lie,' and tagged on despondently, 'before. Says his sleep was disturbed.'

'Ah-huh. You know Brady well, right?'

'Yeah,' Jackson confirmed. 'Since he was a nipper.'

'Sound sleeper?' the Pinkerton man probed. Saul Jackson's silence answered Crane's question. 'So it isn't likely that a prowler in your hen-house would wake him, is it?'

Crane's smile reeked with satisfaction.

'There's still no proof that Willie robbed and killed Henry Jasper,' Jackson flung back.

Coldly, the Pinkerton agent replied, 'I figure that a man up and about on the kind of flimsy story which Brady supplied as a reason for his prowling is a good basis for suspicion, Marshal Jackson.'

There were no words Jackson could utter in contradiction of Crane's assertion.

The Pinkerton detective's next question was, 'Can you trust the men you've assigned to stop leavers?'

'Yes.'

'Then I think we should go talk to Willie Brady, Marshal.' He sighed heavily. 'If he's still around for talking to, that is.'

'Talk all you like, Crane,' Jackson flung back. 'Willie played no part in Jasper's demise!'

Hawk Crane was at the law-office door when he launched a thunderbolt.

'The proceeds of the robbery would, in time, if he's smart enough to let the dust settle, set him up in that freighting business that he's been so keen on starting up.'

Jackson's face set in stone.

'As I hear it, robbery was about the only way that Willie Brady would get his hands on the money he needed, Marshal.'

The lawman cast about for a countering retort but hopelessly floundered, unable to contradict the logic of the Pinkerton detective's reasoning. All he could say was, 'You've been busy, Mr Crane.'

Crane smiled smugly. 'It's what keeps a Pinkerton ahead of the game, Marshal.'

When Willie Brady rode into the ranch yard, Luke Harper, sitting on the corral fence watching a rider trying to break the spirit of a bucking mustang, turned his attention to Willie. The rancher closely scrutinized the young man's appearance, and saw the signs of a drinking-bout in the puffy skin of his cheeks and in the hollows of his eyes. But, other than that, he seemed to be in fine fettle, and Harper was both relieved and pleased that he had made it back to the Broken Wheel, more or less intact.

Dismounting, Willie apologized, 'Sorry 'bout my harin' off the way I did yesterday, Mr Harper. It was a damn fool thing to do, sir.'

Luke Harper had an urge to reach out and draw Willie Brady into his arms, but not being a demonstrative man, he found the action beyond his reach.

'Well, now that you've graced us with your presence,' the rancher said gruffly, 'maybe you'll do the chores you left undone in your madcap dash to town yesterday.'

'And more,' Willie promised the rancher. 'And 'fore I forget, Marshal Jackson said for you to head for town to bring Jesse home, 'fore he gets himself in a mess of trouble.'

Harper shook his head sadly. 'What devil's got into Jesse, Willie?'

'Oh, Jesse ain't bad, Mr Harper. He's just goin' through one of them wild sprees fellas go through now and then. He'll be just fine, I reckon.'

Grasping at straws, the rancher asked, 'You think so, Willie?'

'I guess I do, Mr Harper.'

Harper grinned at the young man's swagger as he strode to the bunkhouse and impulsively called, 'Use the privy in the house to spruce up, Willie.'

'Huh?' Willie responded, wide-eyed.

No one had ever seen the ranch house's swish indoor privy, but everyone had speculated about how the fancy rig might look. Now he was about to set eyes on it. Heck, it would be akin to getting a glimpse of the Garden of Eden!

'But take your boots off before you enter the house,' the rancher instructed.

Harper's grin went from ear to ear as he watched Willie's swagger take on the proportions of a Mexican grandee as he headed for the house, hollering along the way to anyone within range that he was sprucing up in the house privy.

It pleased the rancher to see Willie so happy and carefree, after the cloud which had hung over him since the day before when he'd had to refuse the young man the help he had sought. Not for the first time, Luke Harper wished that Willie Brady was his flesh and blood; a wish he had had even before Jesse turned bad.

Thoughts of better days flooded back to occupy the rancher's mind, when his wife Mary was alive and Jesse would regale them of an evening with his impersonations of neighbours and friends that would have them laughing heartily, so accurate an impersonator was he, and still was to this day. He recalled fondly one particular Sunday afternoon, when Saul and Martha Jackson had visited, and Jesse did an impression of the marshal which, if a body closed his eyes, a body would have sworn was Jackson himself talking. His amazement overcome, Saul Jackson had laughed heartily at the cheeky impersonation.

'Hell, I'd best head for town, I guess,' Luke Harper said wearily. 'Not that Jesse will pay any heed to my wishes.'

About a mile from the ranch, Harper's trail crossed Jackson's and Crane's.

'Howdy, Luke,' the marshal greeted warmly.

'Where're you headed, Saul?' the rancher asked Jackson.

'As it happens, the Broken Wheel'

'The Broken Wheel? What for?'

The Oakville marshal introduced Hawk Crane.

'A pleasure, sir,' said Crane, shaking the rancher's hand.

Preoccupied with his own concerns, the rancher reminded the marshal, 'You didn't answer my question, Saul.'

'Me and Mr Crane need to talk to Willie Brady, Luke.'

Flashing alarm lit the rancher's eyes.

'Willie? Is he in some kind of trouble?'

Pointedly, his glance sliding Crane's way, Jackson said, 'Don't reckon so, Luke.'

Harper glanced at Crane with a keen curiosity.

'Mr Crane is a Pinkerton detective,' the Oakville marshal informed the rancher.

Harper's watery blue eyes glinted with interest. Though still barely out of swaddling, the Pinkerton Detective Agency had become something of a legend in the West, having been instrumental in corralling a bevy of hardcases whom the law had not had any success in bringing to book. A Pinkerton man was a respected man; impeccable character being the hallmark of the Pinkerton operatives.

'Don't want to seem rude or prying, Mr Crane,' the rancher said. 'But what call is there in these parts for the services of a Pinkerton detective?'

Jackson filled Harper in on Ashley Bryant's misfortune.

The rancher's response was one of scoffing laughter. 'Can't say that I have any sympathy for that vulture, Ashley Bryant! Though I am sorry that an innocent man died trying to guard his ill-gotten gains.'

Hawk Crane's right eyebrow arched. 'You don't like Mr Bryant, sir?'

'Hate his damn guts!' Harper ranted. 'Be hard to find a rancher in this valley who doesn't.'

'Oh?'

Harper fumed – he always did at mention of Ashley Bryant. 'A couple of years back this valley suffered drought. Men were left with hollow-sided stock, no feed and dry streams. Bryant saw his chance to take advantage. Offered loans at rates of interest that, in the long run, no man could afford to meet. A lot of the smaller outfits folded up – some bigger ones too. Left the valley with only the clothes on their backs, while that snake Bryant moved on to their range.'

The rancher's tirade continued:

'Sorry about this feller Jasper, Mr Crane. Be better if it was Ashley Bryant whose throat was cut!'

Hawk Crane thoughtfully watched the worry-hunched Harper into the distance. The rancher was weighed down with another worry about Willie Brady, on recollection of the young man's angry departure for town the day before, after he had refused him the loan he needed to start up the freight line he'd been talking about running since he was knee-high. Now Ashley Bryant had been robbed. And that was the lesser trouble, compared to murder. The rancher would bet his last dime on Willie Brady being unable to perpetrate such a foul deed. But he also knew that desperate men did desperate deeds. A ranch hand, arriving back from town the day before, had brought the news of Lucy Webster having broken her ties to Willie, and that she would not bind herself to him again unless he could marry her. Lucy was a much sought after woman – Ashley Bryant for one would have her on his arm any day as a trophy. If Lucy wanted to get off that shelf she imagined herself sitting on, there would be no shortage of willing arms to catch her.

Worry like that could unhinge a man; even an above-the-board fella like Willie Brady.

'Forget what you're thinking,' Jackson advised Crane. 'Luke Harper is the straightest arrow I've ever known.' The marshal urged his horse on. ''Sides, he wasn't in town.'

'Didn't have to be.'

Jackson drew rein.

Crane elaborated. 'In my experience as a Pinkerton man, murder can be done from a distance, Marshal. Luke Harper could be the arranger rather than the doer. Same thing in my book.' His gaze settled on Jackson. 'In the law's book, too.'

The Oakville marshal dismissed Hawk Crane's thinking out of hand.

'For a man to do what you're thinking, he'd have to have a twisted sort of brain. Luke Harper hasn't got that kind of mind!'

'He's sure angry enough,' the Pinkerton detective persisted. 'And I've known less pressing motives for murder than crippling interest rates. A man burdened with the kind of rates Ashley Bryant apparently applies might very well see a whole lot of joy in robbing him of his money. A man might figure that he was only taking back his own.'

'And murder?' Jackson growled

'Murder became part of the deal when Henry Jasper just happened to get in the way.'

Jackson reasoned, 'Lots of men get angry. That doesn't mean they're killers.'

Crane shrugged. 'If Harper owes Bryant big time . . .?'

Snorting dismissively, Saul Jackson again urged his horse forward. Hawk Crane fell in alongside him.

'Harper's a desperate man, Marshal.'

'Men get angry and desperate, too,' retorted Jackson. 'But like I said—'

'I know what you said, Marshal,' the Pinkerton

agent interjected. 'Harper's the straightest arrow you've ever known.'

Conversation died for a spell, before Hawk Crane returned to gnaw at the bone again.

'Just exactly how strong is Ashley Bryant's throttle-hold on Harper?'

Testily, Jackson said, 'Luke Harper's affairs aren't for discussion.'

Equally testy, Crane replied, 'Every man-jack's affairs are up for discussion, Marshal Jackson. Murder and robbery's been committed.'

It took a while for Saul Jackson's ire to lose its spikes, but when it did he had to admit that under the circumstances, Hawk Crane was right.

'I'd say Bryant's close on getting his hands on the Broken Wheel,' he said.

'Motive, I'd say, wouldn't you?'

The Pinkerton detective now really had a bone to chew on. For Jackson's part, and much to his shame, his thoughts began to drift along the path that Crane's theorizing had opened up. The rancher's rage with his growing predicament of meeting Bryant's exorbitant loan repayments grew by the day, as he watched the Broken Wheel fade away.

Hawk Crane's next statement gave Jackson no comfort.

'Losing what a man's slaved to build, can often make an honest man do things he never thought he would do.'

In a lifetime as a badge-toter, Saul Jackson knew only too well the veracity of the Pinkerton detective's claim.

TEN

'He's in the house!'

'In Mr Harper's personal privy, too!' a second man added, gawping.

The answers were in response to Jackson's enquiry as to Willie Brady's whereabouts. The marshal headed for the house.

The first man asked, 'Hey, Marshal Jackson. Will ya tell us if the privy's got flushin' water?'

The second said, ''Cause we can't trust that Willie Brady to tell us the darn truth; him jibin' us all the time the way he does.'

A third man added, 'Will ya, Marshal?'

Jackson chuckled. 'I'll draw you fellas a map, OK?'

When Jackson opened the ranch house door, Willie Brady's tuneless singing greeted him. The marshal winced. Never had he known a man with a scratchier voice. Brady's singing was like needles being drawn across a blacksmith's anvil.

I got me a woman in Tennessee
Sweet as honey, stings like a bee
Love her dearly, love her true
But she don't want no hobo blues.
I—

Jackson's teeth twanged, as Willie cut loose with a wailing note that must have had every cat in the territory headed for Mexico.

got me a woman in Arkansas
Cute as a button, pretty as a bow
Love her dearly, love her true—

Jackson slapped his hands over his ears as Willie's rasping, nasal tones filled every inch of the house.

But she don't want no hobo blues
I—

'Willie,' Jackson hailed, 'stop your caterwauling, unless you want the dead to walk!'

'Marshal Jackson?'

'It's me.' He started upstairs. 'Are you decent?'

'No,' Willie called back. 'But I got lots of soap

where it matters!'

'Wait,' Jackson ordered Hawk Crane, as he started up the stairs behind him. 'I reckon Willie will talk easier to me.'

Crane, though not liking being excluded, saw the sense in the marshal's reasoning.

'Coming in, Willie,' Jackson called out.

He opened the bathroom door.

'Howdy, Marshal,' Willie Brady greeted.

Jackson was awestruck on seeing what had become known in the valley as the Harper Privy, and it was even more grand and ornate than folk had speculated, with a bath long and deep enough to bathe a man's horse in, with fancy taps, the likes of which he'd never set eyes on before.

'Somethin', ain't it?' Willie said, still in awe of his luxurious surroundings himself. 'Flush the privy, Marshal,' he invited. 'No lyin', water spurts right out from under the darn rim! I tell ya, it's a wonder to behold.'

Unable to resist his curiosity, Jackson flushed, and stepped back startled as a strange gurgling sound came from the privy and water gushed from under the rim of the porcelain rig, as Willie had predicted; Jackson scratched his head.

'I'll be . . .'

'Ain't it a wonder?' Willie sighed.

'That it is,' the lawman agreed. Then, shaking off his amazement of the Harper Privy, he said,

'Willie, we've got to talk, official like.'

'Official like? I ain't done nothin'. What d'ya want to talk 'bout?'

Saul Jackson was facing one of the hardest and least palatable moments of his life. 'About Henry Jasper's murder, and Ashley Bryant's cash, Willie.'

ELEVEN

Willie Brady, seated in the parlour, had as much colour in his cheeks as a week-old corpse. 'That's loco talk,' he gasped, in response to Hawk Crane's outlining of what he reckoned to be the circumstances of Henry Jasper's demise. 'I never killed Mr Jasper! Nor stole Ashley Bryant's money neither!' Willie looked in desperation to Saul Jackson. 'You don't believe any of this, do you, Marshal?' he pleaded.

'No, I don't, Willie. But Mr Crane has the right to think as he's thinking, not knowing you as I do. And I'd have to admit that if I were in his shoes. Well . . .'

'There was no chicken-thief, was there, Brady?' the Pinkerton man pounced.

'There was, too.'

'You're lying!' Crane growled. 'You needed an excuse to be up and about when you arrived back from murdering Henry Jasper and bumped into the marshal.'

'That ain't the way it was,' Willie Brady groaned.

The Pinkerton man showed no mercy, nor gave any quarter.

'You needed money. Lord knows you bothered everyone you could to get it. You told everyone that you'd get the money to start up that freight line you've been dreaming about. And you were outside the Golden Plate cafe yesterday when Bryant was discussing his plans with a friend to have money conveyed back East.'

Jackson had a sneaking admiration for Crane's thoroughness, and the Pinkerton code of leaving no stone unturned.

Willie's eyes flashed pleadingly to Jackson. The marshal's heart went out to the young man, but as the law in Oakville, with a sworn duty to snare wrongdoers, he had to let Crane get answers from Willie Brady, good or bad.

The Pinkerton detective shoved his face right into Willie's. 'You needed cash, Brady. And you grabbed your chance to get it!'

'Ain't so!' Willie whined.

'Best if you confess now,' Crane advised. 'Because I'm going to hound you until you do. Now, we'll start again.'

Jackson stepped in.

'Willie's given his answers for now, Crane.'

Thwarted, the Pinkerton agent accused, 'Helping a friend out of a fix, Marshal?'

Hawk Crane was tumbled across the room by the marshal's hammer-blow. 'Like I said,' he grated. 'Willie's given his answers for now.'

The Pinkerton man hauled himself off the floor, feeling his jaw and staggering dizzily. He warned, 'I think your friend is guilty, Marshal. I aim to see him hang for Henry Jasper's murder.'

The Oakville lawman said, 'I hold a contrary view. But I promise you that if Willie Brady is guilty, he'll sure as hell hang high!' He turned to a trembling Willie Brady. 'You stay put right here 'til Jasper's killer is found, Willie.'

Crane cribbed, 'You're giving him the chance to hightail it, Marshal. It'll be too late to come looking when his dust has settled.'

Grudgingly, Jackson had to concede the logic of Crane's reasoning.

'I guess Mr Crane's got a point, Willie. Saddle up. You're coming to town.'

Willie asked Jackson in disbelief, 'You're jailing me?'

'Don't see what else I can do, Willie.'

On the ride back to town, their trail crossed Luke and Jesse Harper's trail on their way back from Oakville. The rancher's eyes took in a downcast

Willie Brady, riding between the marshal and the Pinkerton detective.

'What's going on, Saul?' the rancher enquired of the marshal.

'Willie's got a cloud hanging over him, Luke, that needs clearing up. It can be best done in town.'

'In jail, you mean,' Willie griped.

'You've arrested Willie?' Jesse Harper asked. 'For the Bryant robbery?'

'And for Henry Jasper's murder,' said Hawk Crane.

Jesse Harper laughed. 'That's loco. Willie wouldn't harm a damn flea. Let alone commit murder!'

'Thanks, Jesse,' Willie said. His glare fixed on Jackson. 'Just as well someone believes I didn't do nothin'.'

Luke Harper said, 'You've got the wrong end of the stick for sure this time, Saul.'

'That's the way I figure too, Luke,' Jackson admitted. 'But as the marshal I've got a duty to hold a man under suspicion. Mr Crane here has the right to insist that I do.'

Jesse Harper promised, 'As soon as I spruce up, I'll be back to town, Marshal. To arrange for Willie's defence against this ridiculous injustice.'

Stern-faced, Jackson replied, 'Don't you reckon you've had enough of town for a spell, Jesse?'

'You're not going to rot in jail, Willie,' the rancher's son promised Brady.

' 'Preciate your kindness, Jesse.'

Luke Harper chipped in, 'We won't let you down, son.'

Willie Brady's glare on Marshal Jackson intensified. 'Just as well I've still got some friends in these parts.'

An hour later, Saul Jackson had to perform the most odious task he had ever had come his way, when he turned the lock in the cell door on Willie Brady.

'Next stop a gallows, Brady,' Hawk Crane crooned smugly.

TWELVE

The second that the Pinkerton agent left to prepare his case for what he was certain would be Willie Brady's trial for murder and robbery, Hank Boothroyd paid Jackson a visit, slipping in silently, Jackson not knowing he was there until he spoke. A ghost would have made more noise.

'What's all this about Willie being a candidate for a rope?' he questioned the marshal sternly. 'Can't say that I like the idea of him being in jail, Marshal.'

Hank Boothroyd having acquainted him with his interest in Willie Brady's welfare, Saul Jackson could understand the gunfighter's concern; it was a worry shared.

'Don't have a choice,' he told Boothroyd. 'As things stand, Willie is the prime suspect for the Pinkerton detective's murder and robbery.'

Boothroyd's eyes flashed towards the cells, and

his thoughts were starkly showing in his glance. 'Busting Willie out of jail won't help, Boothroyd,' said Jackson.

'He's not having a noose put round his neck, that's for sure,' the gunfighter threatened. Boothroyd's hand dropped to hover over his gun.

'Willie has to remain in jail until this ruckus is sorted out,' said Jackson.

'And if I don't agree?' Hank Boothroyd said, with quiet menace.

Jackson said, 'I don't believe Willie's harmed a fly. But I have to get proof, Boothroyd. Until I do, Willie stays in jail!' His gaze was unflinching as he asked, 'Where were you last night, mister?'

'Sleeping.'

'Hotel?'

'Livery.'

'Livery, huh,' the Oakville lawman pondered. 'Horses don't talk. A man could pretty much come and go as he pleased, sleeping in the livery.'

'I'm not a thief, Marshal,' the gunfighter said. 'Never stole a cent.'

Saul Jackson remained unflinching. 'Don't know about being a thief. But you are a killer, Boothroyd.'

The gunfighter's anger flared.

'I never snuck up on a man like Jasper's killer did!'

From what Jackson had heard of Hank

Boothroyd's style, he could take his fiery statement as fact. The marshal grabbed his hat. 'I'd better go and turn some rocks, I guess.'

'Anything I can do?' Boothroyd asked.

Jackson answered bluntly, 'No,' but quickly changed his mind. 'You could keep the prisoner company for a spell. Act as my unofficial deputy.'

The gunfighter's smile was richly wry. 'You're not scared that I'll bust Willie out, Marshal?'

'Not yet,' Jackson replied, wearily. 'But I figure that if Willie Brady's future is not looking rosy, you'll try later.' Jackson paused in the open door. 'Then, Boothroyd, I'll have to stop you. And that, for Willie's sake, would surely pain me.'

'Stop me?' The gunfighter's features set in stone. 'You think you could, Marshal?'

'I'll damn well try,' Jackson returned spiritedly.

'It's likely I'd kill you?' Boothroyd drawled.

'Likely you would,' the Oakville lawman conceded. Then a cocky smile crossed his lips. 'Then, again, maybe you wouldn't.'

Hank Boothroyd's smile was lazy. 'I guess we'll just have to wait and see how things pan out, eh, Marshal?'

Saul Jackson's gaze was steady. 'I guess we will at that, eh, Mr Boothroyd.'

Leaving the law-office, Jackson took a moment to gather his thoughts. He had told the gunfighter that he had some rocks to turn, but the problem was where to find those rocks. Not being a trained detective, like Hawk Crane, he'd have to rummage about, likely tripping over the solution to the case rather than unmasking the killer by the application of logic and deduction like a Pinkerton man would. But in his time he had sent many killers to the gallows. He was determined that this time, with the stakes so high, he would not fail Willie Brady. He would see to it that the right man, the guilty man, would stand in the shadow of a hangman's noose.

THIRTEEN

Martha Jackson came hurrying to the door to quiz her husband about Willie Brady's incarceration. Jackson had specifically dropped by the house to ease her fears, the town buzzing as it was with the news that Willie was Henry Jasper's murderer.

Taking her in his arms, the lawman consoled his weeping wife. 'It's all right, Martha. Willie isn't going to be in jail for long.' Recalling the knots of dour-faced men gathering around town, eyeing the jail, he concluded, 'Jail is the safest place for Willie right now.'

'Willie Brady is the kindest, gentlest soul I know, Saul,' Martha Jackson said. 'How could people think of him as a killer?'

The marshal saved his wife the evidence piled up against Willie Brady. He said, 'Got to go. I've got things to do, Martha.' He promised, 'I'll drop by later.' He pecked his wife on the cheek and hurried away, headed for the Silver Eagle hotel.

'I'll bake a pie for Willie, and take it to him,' Martha Jackson promised.

'You do that, Martha,' her husband said. 'One of your pies will surely lift Willie's spirits.'

On his way back to the hotel Jackson observed the brooding mood of the citizens, particularly outside the Happy Lizard, where the hangers-on who had formed around Jesse Harper, now at a loose end with Jesse gone back to the Broken Wheel, were lapping at Brent's heels, and taking on board his rabble-rousing. His guff as the marshal went by was measured for him to hear.

'The way I figure, that murdering cur Willie Brady should be strung up right now.'

Jackson paid no visible heed to Brent's trouble-stirring, figuring that taking the bait was what would benefit Brent most. But he worried that Brent's considerable skills as a street orator would fire up others outside his immediate circle. That would mean big trouble. If he fired up the different groups of men hanging around looking for leadership, pretty soon a lynch mob would haul Willie Brady from jail and serve up the worst kind of Western justice.

The quick rope and short branch kind of justice!

It worried Jackson too, that he could not be in

all places at the same time. The town had suffered a slump in prosperity since the dry season of a few years before, and would take time to recover. Meanwhile, the town had meagre resources, town taxes being down. Its coffers were not flush enough to pay a deputy's salary.

Jackson found himself in the unenviable position of having to rely on a gunfighter to watch his back. 'Can't you ask that Pinkerton detective to help you clear Willie's name?' Martha had suggested hopefully.

He hadn't the heart to tell her that the man she was putting her trust in as Willie Brady's saviour, was the very man who was preparing to send him to the gallows!

FOURTEEN

Jesse Harper slowly opened the bunkhouse door, wincing as it creaked. He cautiously poked his head out, eyes darting, before he slipped out and quickly sought the cover at the side of the bunkhouse. The structure was backed up against rock, whose rear and sides formed a wind-breaking cocoon in winter, and now an equally safe refuge for Harper while he reconnoitered the ranch yard. He waited until he was certain that there were no watching eyes. Satisfied, he hurried back to the ranch house, smiling craftily. But certain as he was that he had not been seen . . .

He had been.

Money being scarce, Luke Harper had had to cut the number of hands he employed, and as a result he had to do many of the tasks that would have normally fallen to a ranch hand to do, like the repair which he was now making to the attic wall, looking out on the bunkhouse.

He wondered about his son's furtive visit to the bunkhouse, but held his tongue. He had just prised Jesse loose from the Happy Lizard's bad influences, and was not of a mind to risk upsetting him and send him haring back to town. There was clear evidence of Saul Jackson's patience wearing thin, and the last thing he wanted was for the marshal, his oldest and dearest friend, to have to crackdown on Jesse. Jackson had already given his son more rope than he had a right to expect, and he was grateful for that, figuring that it was only a matter of time before Jesse got himself together again. Doing or saying anything that would pitch Jesse back into the cauldron that was Oakville right now, would not do him or Saul Jackson any favours. Of course, Jesse was going back to town to arrange for Willie Brady's defence, as he had promised he would. But once those arrangements had been made, he had promised to turn round and head back to the Broken Wheel.

Jesse appeared to be much at ease with himself now, and Luke Harper was hopeful that his recent waywardness was at an end.

Thinking about how to save Willie Brady's hide, Marshal Jackson had decided to retrace events, right from the time Willie had come running that morning, claiming that he had given chase to a chicken-rustler.

However, standing in his own hen-house, his faith in finding a direction that would lead to Willie Brady's acquittal of the suspicions, and soon-to-be charges against him, faded, until he stepped on a Happy Lizard playing chip. He picked up the chip and rolled it between his fingers. What did it mean? Probably nothing, he concluded. Sometimes he played cards at the Happy Lizard; the chip was probably his. He could have dropped it from his pocket when he had been feeding the hens. But then had he ever been so flush as to be able to ignore cashing in a five-dollar chip? Could the chip belong to the chicken-rustler of whom Willie spoke?

Saul Jackson let his thoughts drift deeper. Normally a thief would not want his presence known. But what if this one did? What if he specifically wanted Willie Brady to give chase? It would have Willie up and about for no good reason. Who would believe his tale about giving chase to a chicken-rustler? In Oakville chicken-rustlers were not a dime a dozen. If rustling was a man's bent, then cows would be his choice. Willie Brady would have been haring about town, just about the time that Henry Jasper had had his throat slit.

Had Willie been cleverly set up?

Jackson focused his thoughts further still. How would the thief and murderer get Willie's attention? An idea leaping to mind, the marshal hurried from the hen-house to examine the grass under the room where Willie Brady had slept.

Alarmed by her husband's madcap antics, Martha Jackson joined her husband just as he gathered up a fistful of pebbles, like those on the path leading to the hen-house. His answer, when she asked him what the stones meant, alarmed her even more.

He said, 'Martha, my darling. I've struck gold!'

Martha Jackson looked at the pebbles in her husband's hand and feared for his sanity.

Hawk Crane hurried to open his room door before the caller hammering on it unhinged it. Saul Jackson pushed past him into the room holding out a handful of stones. Crane looked at the stones, puzzled, and then at Jackson for an explanation which he hoped would not be as loco as the lawman's antics.

'These are what woke Willie Brady,' Jackson declared. 'How many times have you slung shale at a window at dead of night, Crane? Maybe to get a lady's attention unknown to her Pa.'

The Pinkerton man was shaking his head.

'You're saying you've never—'

Crane interjected, sternly, 'What cock-an'-bull yarn are you trying to spin me, Marshal Jackson?'

'It's not a yarn,' the Oakville lawman growled. 'Someone who wanted to have the blame for the robbery and murder to fall on Willie Brady's shoulders, slung shale at his window to wake him up. Knowing that when he saw what he thought was a chicken-rustler, he'd give chase.'

'The point being?'

'To have Willie haring around town just about the time that Henry Jasper's throat was slit.'

The Pinkerton detective looked at Jackson as if he'd grown a second head. 'You're offering me a handful of stones as proof of Willie Brady's innocence?'

'Stones I found in the grass under Willie Brady's window. The same stones as on the path leading to my hen-house.'

On hearing his evidence, Jackson knew how flimsy it was; it was no evidence at all. He had hoped to shake Hawk Crane's conviction that it was Willie who had robbed and killed Henry Jasper. Clearly, he had not. In fact, judging by Crane's disbelieving reaction, all he had done was strengthen the Pinkerton agent's resolve to see Willie Brady swing, resolve to resist what he saw as the marshal's efforts to save his friend's neck.

The detective shook his head in dismissal of the lawman's evidence.

'I could reach out anywhere in this town and pick up a handful of shale, Marshal Jackson. That's not proof you're holding. That's hope.'

Jackson rooted in his vest-pocket for the Happy Lizard playing-chip. 'This was in my hen-house, too.'

'So?' the Pinkerton agent drawled.

'Means a frequenter of the Happy Lizard paid a visit.'

'You play cards, Marshal?'

Grudgingly, Jackson admitted, 'Now and then.'

'You play with chips?'

'Now and then.'

'Happy Lizard chips?'

'Sometimes.'

Jackson knew what was coming next.

'And you visit your hen-house, don't you?'

'Seems to me, Crane,' Jackson flared, 'that you've set your cap on Willie Brady being guilty, and you don't want to look anywhere else for the killer.'

Grimly, the Pinkerton detective said, 'That makes us men with something in common, Marshal. I want Willie Brady's neck in a noose – you don't. I'll do anything to put him on a gallows – you'll do anything to stop me. You see him as a friend. I see him as a murderer.' Hawk Crane crossed the room to come face to face with Saul Jackson. 'I figure that's an accurate statement of where we stand, Marshal Jackson.'

Jackson did not have a rebuff for the Pinkerton detective's assessment of the situation, because there was no denying the truth of it.

'I've been thinking, Marshal . . .'

'I bet you have,' Jackson growled.

'I figure, if we look, we'll find Ashley Bryant's money stashed some place on the Broken Wheel ranch. Where I think Willie Brady hid it.'

The Pinkerton agent's eyes locked with Jackson's.

'I think we should ride out there, right now, Marshal Jackson. If we find the money . . .'

There was no need to finish his statement. Its meaning was abundantly clear. Should they find Bryant's dollars at the ranch, Willie Brady's neck would be in a noose faster than he could blink!

FIFTEEN

Leaving the hotel, Jackson was faced with a sour-faced, liquored-up mob led by Johnny Brent blocking his path. Brent challenged, 'You gotta killer in the caboose, Marshal. This citizens' committee figure that Willie Brady should be strung up. We aim to see justice done!'

The marshal scoffed. 'Citizens' committee?' His angry eyes swept the town scum facing him. 'Go back to your bottles, gents. Leave the law-keeping to me.'

A wispy man who spent his time sitting on Brent's coat-tails in the hope of licking up the drops that spilled from his glass, whined, 'Heck, Marshal. You ain't goin' to hang no friend o' yours.'

Jackson vowed, 'If Willie Brady is guilty, he'll hang like any other man.'

'You 'spect us to believe that?' Brent sniggered.

'I don't give a damn whether you do or not, Brent. Or any other man of you either.' Jackson's hand hovered over his sixgun. 'Now, step aside.'

All eyes were on Johnny Brent. The marshal hoped that if he stood firm, the citizens' committee would vanish faster than snow on flame. If he won, Brent would be the loser. His pride would be dented; his sway over the town dregs ended.

The seconds ticked heavily by as Brent tussled with his cowardice and pride. Saul Jackson welcomed Jesse Harper's intervention.

'Back off boys!' The rancher's son climbed out of the saddle and hitched his horse to the Happy Lizard rail. 'Do as the marshal says, Johnny.'

Brent was frankly puzzled. 'I thought this is what you'd want, Jesse?'

'Well it isn't!' Harper snapped. 'Now back off!' Jesse Harper pushed his way through the mob to join Jackson on the hotel porch to declare, 'I stand with Marshal Jackson on this one. Willie Brady, guilty or not, is entitled to a fair trial.'

His confusion deepening more by the second, Brent mumbled, 'If that's the way you want it, Jesse.'

'That's the way I want it,' the rancher's son confirmed. He laughed good-humouredly. 'The drinks are on me.'

The mob instantly broke up, thirsty tongues

licking dry lips. Brent hung back, glowering at Jesse Harper.

'I've arranged for John Benjamin to represent Willie at his trial,' the rancher's son informed Jackson.

There were two lawyers in Oakville, one good, one bad. John Benjamin was the good one, and charged accordingly for his services.

'Mighty generous of you, Jesse,' the marshal said.

'Willie deserves, and might I add needs, the best, Marshal Jackson. I'm just happy that I can help out.'

Jesse chuckled, and began an inch-perfect impersonation of John Benjamin in the lawyer's mellifluous tone. 'Your honour. In the matter of William Richard Brady . . .'

In fact, so good was Jesse Harper's impersonation of the lawyer, it stopped Benjamin, who was crossing the street, dead in his tracks. To everyone's amusement, John Benjamin said, 'Jesse, if I ever need a lawyer, I'll hire you.'

The amusing interlude over, Jackson strolled to his horse. 'You headed out of town, Marshal?' Harper enquired.

'The marshal and me are headed for the Broken Wheel, Mr Harper,' Hawk Crane said, coming from the hotel. 'I figure that's where we'll find Ashley Bryant's dollars.'

Agape, Jesse Harper said, 'At the Broken Wheel?'

Crane said, 'That's where I figure Willie Brady's stashed the proceeds of his foul deed.'

The rancher's son opined, 'I'd say that you fellas are on a wild-goose chase.'

'Why so?' Jackson asked.

Jesse Harper's attitude was scoffing. 'Willie hasn't got the brains for murder and robbery, Marshal Jackson.'

Jackson asked, 'You figure that a fella's got to be smart to commit murder, huh, Jesse?'

'Not to commit it, no.' Jackson noted the swagger that came into Jesse's gait. 'But to get away with it, yes.'

The marshal pointed his horse to the south end of Main. 'Interesting talking with you, Jesse,' he said. He rode away, his face reflecting the thoughts piling up in his head.

His first port of call was Wes Flatley's infirmary to enquire about Lil Scannell's progress. Doc Flatley had worked a miracle. He found the raven-haired saloon dove much improved, but restless.

'She'll pull through,' the medico told Jackson.

'Mighty restless,' noted Jackson.

'Soon as I can, when Lil is a little more mended, I'll ride over to Bitter Creek to borrow some sleeping-potion from Nathan Cross, until I can get a supply myself.' Wes Flatley scratched his beard. 'Thought I had some right here,' he looked to a glass medicine-cabinet. 'Guess I'm getting old and forgetful, Saul.'

'You've done a fine job, Wes,' the marshal complimented. He was at the infirmary door when he paused and turned to ask, 'Has Jesse Harper visited?'

'Yes. Last night. Late, too,' the sawbones grumbled. 'All dewy-eyed. Sat for a spell with Lil.'

'Alone?'

'No.'

Saul Jackson's shoulders slumped. 'Be seeing you, Wes.'

'Except while I went and brewed coffee.'

The marshal turned around.

'A show of bad manners, if you ask me. Jesse walking out like he did when I took the trouble.'

Saul Jackson thoughtfully glanced at the glass medicine-cabinet.

Continuing along Main, his thoughts deeper still, the lawman drew rein outside the law-office. 'Got a chore to do,' he told Hawk Crane. 'Won't take a minute.'

He entered the law-office, opened a desk drawer and took out a Bible. Then he headed straight for the cells where he found Hank Boothroyd talking and laughing with Willie Brady.

'Glad you've stuck around,' Jackson greeted

the gunfighter. 'Stand up. A man can't take an oath sitting down.'

To his utter amazement, Boothroyd had the Bible shoved in his hand.

'Say after me; I swear by Almighty God—'

Hank Boothroyd found his tongue.

'What the hell is this, Marshal?'

'Plain, I thought. I'm swearing you in as my deputy.'

Willie Brady cried, 'But Mr Boothroyd is a gunfighter, Marshal.'

Jackson said, 'The way this town is bubbling, that's exactly what we need.' Addressing Boothroyd, he explained, 'I've got to ride out of town. I need a deputy in my absence to uphold the law and to protect my prisoner from harm.' Saul Jackson's eyes locked with the gunfighter's. 'I figured, Mr Boothroyd, that you'd want the job.'

Hank Boothroyd glanced at Willie Brady. 'You reckoned right, Marshal.'

Jackson finished the oath, and told Boothroyd, 'You'll find a deputy's badge in the desk drawer.'

'I'll be danged,' was Willie Brady's comment as the marshal departed.

Outside, the lawman vaulted into the saddle. 'Let's go, Crane.'

Hawk Crane was knocked back on his heels when Hank Boothroyd came to the law-office door polishing a deputy's badge.

*

No conversation passed between the men on the ride to the Broken Wheel. The Pinkerton detective had tried to strike up a conversation to pass the time, but he soon tired of trying against Jackson's lack of interest. So deep in thought was the marshal that Crane reckoned he could shout right in his ear and not disturb his thinking.

Luke Harper saw Jackson and Crane ride across the flat plain to the house. He was at the front door to greet them when they arrived.

'What brings you gents out this way again?' the rancher enquired.

Stepping down from his horse, the marshal informed the rancher, 'Mr Crane wants to search the ranch, Luke.'

'Search the ranch?'

A sudden fear gripped the rancher.

Jackson said, 'He reckons he'll find the loot from the robbery here.'

'At the Broken Wheel?' Harper asked indignantly.

'I've got my reasons, if you want to hear them, sir,' said Hawk Crane.

Harper said, 'Best come in the house, I guess.'

Luke Harper listened dourly as the Pinkerton detective explained. 'If we find nothing, then I reckon that'll be a plus for Brady. On the other hand, if we find Ashley Bryant's money . . .'

The rancher was as uneasy as a cat sitting on hot coals.

Saul Jackson said, 'I guess, Luke, that one way or the other this search needs to be done.'

As the marshal and Crane began their search, the Pinkerton man observed, 'Judging by Harper's reaction just now, he thinks every bit as highly of Willie Brady as you do, Marshal.'

'Probably more,' Jackson said, recalling the rancher's sterling endorsement of Willie. But he was not at all sure that Willie Brady's wellbeing was the primary reason for Luke Harper's discomfort at having the Broken Wheel searched.

The skittering thoughts that had been occupying Saul Jackson's mind were, he reckoned, beginning to make sense.

SIXTEEN

The search of the ranch did not take long before it brought results. Hawk Crane came triumphantly from the bunkhouse, holding aloft a bundle of bills.

'Told you,' he smugly boasted to Jackson. 'Found these under Willie Brady's bunk. He didn't even bother to properly replace the floorboard he'd prised loose.'

'I figure that Willie is falling through that gallows trap-door a mite too conveniently,' the lawman opined. He took the bundle of bills from Crane. 'What do you reckon's here? A couple of thousand dollars? Why didn't Willie hide the entire stash in the same hidey-hole, you figure?'

'You don't give up, do you?' Crane snarled. He grabbed back the bills, and waving the bundle in Jackson's face declared, 'This is enough to put Willie Brady's neck in a noose for sure!'

Luke Harper worriedly watched the interplay between the two men from the parlour window, acutely conscious of having seen Jesse sneak from the bunkhouse only a couple of hours before. The Pinkerton agent had found what he was looking for. Willie Brady was in the most immediate peril.

The rancher cast his mind back to the fat saddle-bags Jesse had taken from his horse on his arrival back at the ranch from town, and he licked parched lips. Was it in Jesse's nature to be a killer? Jesse had got on to a slippery slope that could end anywhere. Had it ended in murder?

Like any father, Luke Harper was loath to believe that his son could be the kind of cold-blooded killer who had murdered Henry Jasper. He began to find reasons, however spurious, to explain away Jesse's bulging saddle-bags and his all-incriminating visit to the bunkhouse.

He went to meet Jackson and Crane as they returned to the house. The Pinkerton detective called out, 'We've got our man, Mr Harper. This bundle of bills was right under Willie Brady's bunk!'

'I guess that's pretty conclusive evidence, sure enough, eh, Saul?' the rancher said.

Jackson held Luke Harper's gaze until the rancher was forced to look away.

'Let's head back to town, Marshal Jackson,'

Crane crowed. He vaulted into his saddle, eager to make tracks. 'We've got a trial to arrange.'

Saul Jackson hung back. He addressed Luke Harper. 'In your heart you know the deck was stacked against Willie, Luke. And I reckon that in your heart you also know who did the stacking. 'Bye, Luke. I trust you to do what's right.'

The rancher said, 'I haven't an idea what you're talking about, Saul.'

Tiredly, the marshal said, 'Sure you do, Luke.' He wheeled his horse and cantered off after Hawk Crane who, in his eagerness to hang Willie Brady, was eating up the trail. 'Sure you do,' he muttered. Saul Jackson left behind in Luke Harper a man tussling with his conscience.

When Jackson arrived back in Oakville, trailing Crane by ten minutes, the town was already buzzing with the Pinkerton detective's news, and a sizeable crowd had gathered outside the law-office. Hank Boothroyd was at the door, Winchester ready, vowing to cut down the first man who tried to get to Willie Brady. Lucy Webster was at the window, in an equally determined mood. On seeing Jackson, the crowd fell back, but only just. The marshal was not in a compromising mood, grimly endorsing the gunfighter's stance.

'There'll be no lynching in my town,' he told the crowd.

A challenging voice rose above the babble of the crowd. Jackson looked to the steps of the Happy Lizard, where Jesse Harper and his cohorts were coming from the saloon. Harper hailed, 'Looks like Willie Brady's as guilty as mortal sin, Marshal.' He shook his head dolefully. 'I'd have bet my last cent on Willie not being a killer.'

'He's not,' the lawman replied stonily. 'You are, Jesse.'

SEVENTEEN

The crowd fell to muffled murmuring.

Harper, getting wind back in his sails fast, scoffed: 'What kind of hooch have you been drinking, Marshal?' To much laughter he shouted, 'Why, it must be worse than the rat's piss that the Happy Lizard serves up!'

Saul Jackson walked to the middle of Main to face Harper. 'I've got to arrest you now, Jesse, for murder and robbery.'

Harper's grin faded. A fearsome black scowl took its place. 'You're loco, Jackson! And I'm not going anywhere.'

Jackson warned, 'Don't be a fool, Jesse. I can take you.'

Harper's bravado faltered, then bounced back. 'I couldn't have killed Henry Jasper.' He called back into the saloon. 'Conchita, honey. Get out here.'

The Mexican saloon dove appeared, sipping whiskey. A man whom she had worked on for an hour trying to prise loose the hefty wallet from his pocket hung tipsily on her arm.

'I'm working, Jesse.'

The rancher's son snorted. 'He'll keep. Tell the marshal where I was last night.'

'With me, Marshal Jackson,' said Conchita.

'All night,' Jesse Harper added.

'That's a fact, Marshal,' one of the mob outside the law-office attested. 'I saw Jesse head upstairs with Conchita 'round midnight.'

The rancher's son swaggered down the Happy Lizard steps, a snide snigger on his lips. 'I guess no matter how you try to get Willie Brady's neck out of a noose, Marshal, it just keeps popping back in.'

Saul Jackson knew that if the bluff he was about to pull did not come off, Jesse Harper would slip the hangman's rope, and Willie Brady, an innocent man, would pay the price for Harper's deed of Cain.

'You drugged Conchita, Jesse,' he charged. 'To give yourself an alibi.'

Jesse Harper's face paled, and his eyes became furtive.

'You gave Conchita that sleeping-potion you stole from Doc Flatley's infirmary last night, when you visited with Lil. That way Conchita would simply assume that when you got into bed with her, and you were still there when she woke up, you had been there all night.'

Jackson closely observed Conchita's thoughtful frown. He prodded, 'I guess you slept really well last night, Conchita. Though maybe your head ached some when you woke up.'

The whore's accusing glance went Jesse Harper's way. The rancher's son swallowed as if his spittle had nails in it.

'Never held with murder, Jesse,' Conchita said angrily.

'Shut up, you tramp!' the rancher's son bellowed.

Jesse Harper's fist swung out to pitch Conchita back through the Happy Lizard bat-wings. The drunken man with her staggered forward, sparking with indignation. Johnny Brent stuck out a leg and tripped him. He crashed down the saloon steps. As he struggled to co-ordinate his legs to stand up, Brent followed through with a boot to the side of the man's head that laid him out cold.

Conchita stumbled back through the saloon's batwings, dazed but furious.

'He beat up on Lil Scannell, too, Marshal Jackson,' she said. 'Came running to my room to get me to spin a yarn for you when you'd come looking.'

'Thank you, Conchita,' the marshal thanked the dove. 'Always figured as much.' He addressed

Harper, 'I'd be obliged if you'd step along to the jail, Jesse.'

'I'm not going to any cage,' he snarled. 'Are you going to take the word of a whore over mine? Luke Harper's son.'

The swelling crowd reacted to Jesse's invocation, truly believing that any son whom the straight-laced rancher had fathered could not be capable of the heinous crimes which the marshal was accusing him of.

Jackson said, 'You know, Jesse, you almost got away with murder. Until I thought of your ability to impersonate anyone.'

Harper's frightened eyes darted at the lawman.

'Thanks to Willie Brady, I got to thinking about why Henry Jasper freely opened the office door. Then I got to figuring that he opened the office door because he thought he was opening it to Ashley Bryant.'

A confused muttering rose from the crowd.

'What kind of rubbish are you spouting, Marshal?' Jesse blustered.

'You're a skilled impersonator, Jesse. When you gave your impersonation of John Benjamin the dime finally dropped,' the marshal resoundingly declared. 'Henry Jasper opened the door to you, Jesse!'

A shocked gasp went up from the crowd, most

of whom were well aware of Jesse Harper's skill as an impersonator. They found the marshal's claim completely plausible.

Though Saul Jackson knew he had Jesse Harper cornered, it gave him no pleasure. He reckoned that in Luke Harper he would lose the best friend a man could ever have.

Lightning-quick, a gun blasted from the middle of Harper's cohorts. Jackson spun around, clutching his left side. The crowd scattered, finding what cover they could. The Broken Wheel ranny who had teamed up with Conchita Murales to fortify Jesse Harper's alibi, which had allowed him to slip the loop for Lil Scannell's beating, broke from the crowd brandishing a smoking Dragoon Colt. He settled the gun on the marshal. Jackson cursed silently that, after facing down some of the toughest *hombres* the West had spawned in his years as a lawman, he was going to die by the gun of a no-consequence snake!

A rifle cracked. The top of the ranny's head exploded. The men around Jesse Harper dived every which way, as a volley of rifle shots tore chunks of wood from the Happy Lizard porch. Jackson looked to where Hank Boothroyd was on one knee outside the law-office, holding a smouldering Winchester. Lucy Webster joined him. Though her shooting was more hopeful than accurate, it served to further scatter Jesse Harper's supporters, most of whom by now had vanished back inside the saloon under a hail of lead and shattering glass.

Jesse Harper stood alone!

EIGHTEEN

Desperate, the rancher's son played his last card.

'Aren't you forgetting something, Marshal?' he blurted out, his nerves twitching. 'You found some of Ashley Bryant's money under Willie Brady's bunk in the Broken Wheel bunkhouse.'

'*Some*?' Jackson drawled.

The marshal's gaze went to Hawk Crane, who had been watching the proceedings from the hotel veranda, and who now confirmed, 'I never said how much we found, Marshal.'

Jackson returned his gaze to Jesse Harper. 'For you to know that only *some* of the stolen money was found under Willie Brady's bunk, *you'd* have to have put it there, Jesse.'

'He did!'

Jackson spun around. Luke Harper was tying his horse to the hitch rail outside the bank. He had always been a quiet-moving man. In the early days, when Oakville was a dream shared with Saul Jackson and a handful of other settlers, his stealthy step had saved many scalps from marauding Indians.

Jackson observed that in the short time since he had seen his friend at the Broken Wheel the years had piled on him, and the life force, which had beaten odds that most men would have succumbed to, had dissipated.

Luke Harper was a man bereft of hope.

'I saw you going into the bunkhouse carrying a parcel, Jesse.' The last of his will for life left him in a weary sigh. 'And I saw you come back out carrying nothing. I guess I knew all along what was in those bulging saddle-bags you left town with this morning, son.'

'What're you saying, Pa?' Jesse Harper bleated.

'I'm telling the truth, Jesse. God knows, I don't want to.' The rancher approached his son. 'I don't know what demon got into you, boy. But it's time you cut his evil out of you, before you meet your Maker.'

'You old fool!' Jesse Harper raged, his eyes dancing with insanity.

Jackson lunged for Luke Harper, but he was too late to prevent Jesse Harper's bullet hitting the rancher. As he fell to the ground with the fatally wounded man, Jesse Harper's Colt tracked him, ready to deliver the same to him.

The rancher pushed the pistol that had fallen from his holster at Jackson. The lawman hesitated.

'Better than the shame of hanging, Saul,' Luke Harper murmured.

Jackson grabbed the gun and fired. The first shot was wild, but had the effect of unsettling Jesse Harper enough to give the lawman a second bite of the cherry. His second bullet caught the rancher's son square in the chest.

'Pa,' Jesse cried out, before toppling forward on to the street. The rancher's fingers reached out to clutch those of his son. 'I'm real sorry, Pa,' he whispered, before his eyes glazed over.

'Someone get Doc Flatley,' Jackson hollered.

'Leave me be, Saul,' said Luke Harper. 'It's best this way.' His fingers fumbled in his vest pocket. He handed the marshal a sheet of parchment. 'It's all legal,' he told him.

Jackson opened and read the last will and testament of Luke Harper, duly signed and witnessed. Amazement spread across Jackson's face. But along with the surprise there was pleasure too.

'Willie Brady will put things right at the Broken Wheel,' the rancher said, contentedly. 'It won't be easy. But he'll have a fine woman in Lucy Webster to help him do it.' Luke Harper's eyes rolled. 'Never figured it would be like this,' he murmured breathlessly. 'Always figured I'd pass on tucked up in that fine four-poster Mary had freighted from San Francisco.'

His smile, the vibrant, fighting smirk that Saul Jackson would remember his friend for, flashed for the briefest of moments before vanishing for ever.

Years, too, piled on Saul Jackson.

FINALE

'Do you, Willie Brady, take this woman, Lucy Webster, to be your—'

'Sure do, Reverend Sweeney!' Willie Brady declared.

'Wait 'til I ask the darn question,' John Sweeney, the travelling preacher who visited Oakville every couple of months, grumbled. 'Things have got to be right in the sight of God before you two go cavorting off!'

'Sorry, Reverend Sweeney,' Willie apologized. 'No offence to God, sir. But I'm sure He'll understand how anxious I am to finally make Lucy my wife.'

Sweeny's whiskey-yellowed eyes settled on Willie, first with disapproval, and then with a benign kindness. 'I guess God will understand all right, young man. Lawful wedded wife . . .?'

'I do, God!' Willie hollered out, testing the roof of the small church with his yell.

It had been a whole year since Willie Brady had taken over as the boss of the Broken Wheel, and he had worked ceaselessly to make the ranch as near as he could to what it had been before misfortune had befallen Luke Harper. A fine herd had brought a good price. Broken Wheel pasture was back to silky greenness, and Willie had displayed, to everyone's astonishment, surprising bookkeeping skills, and a keen talent for renegotiating the terms of his mortgage with Ashley Bryant, after many hot-tempered squabbles from which a mutual respect had grown.

He was making steady inroads in his debt to the Oakville bank, too, and Andrew Benton, the bank president, had agreed to extend the period for repayment at a moderate rate of interest, to the other side of a new herd which Willie was fattening.

The opinion in Oakville was that Luke Harper had chosen wisely and well in Willie Brady to see the continuation and new prosperity of the Broken Wheel ranch.

Saul Jackson had handed in his badge, having been left with no heart for the law. The Pinkerton detective agency, on Hawk Crane's say-so, had offered him a post in recognition of the keen as mustard detective work which had unmasked

Henry Jasper's murderer. He had declined to follow an ambition he had held for a long time; that of being a restaurateur.

He had, with no small amount of help from Willie Brady, built and stocked a new hen-house, and with Martha, had opened a café which served chicken as its main menu. As yet, the Clucking Egg was not having much success, but there was no denying that more of its tables at lunch-time were being occupied.

'I might have to ditch those four-legged critters m'self soon,' Willie Brady had joked on a recent visit, on seeing over half the tables taken.

Saul Jackson knew that there was little chance of chicken becoming the main diet in cow country. But he was happy enough with his lot.

Sometimes, from far-flung places, he received a letter from Hank Boothroyd; the latest from Peru. He had hung up his gun, and had taken a wife. At such times, his thoughts would go back to the day the gunfighter had left Oakville.

'Why didn't you tell Willie that you were his rightful father, Hank?' Jackson had asked.

Boothroyd had hung around town mulling for a couple of weeks after the terrible events of Luke and Jesse Harper's demise; weeks in which Jackson had formed a friendship with the gunfighter.

'That time I spent in the jail gabbing with

Willie,' he had explained, 'He did nothing but talk about his Pa. Saw him as some kind of saint. I didn't have the heart to set him straight and tell him that I was his real father, and not Sam Brady. Figured it was a secret best kept, Saul.'

As Hank Boothroyd had ridden away from Oakville, Jackson figured that Willie Brady was a very lucky fella to have had two men who were very proud of him as a son. And two more, himself and Luke Harper, who would have been equally proud to be able to say that he was theirs.

A full moon was shining on Willie Brady's wedding-night when, with his new wife, he placed a bunch of wildflowers on the side-by-side graves on the Broken Wheel's shaded south pasture where Luke and Jesse Harper rested. Together they prayed for Luke and Jesse, and gave thanks to Luke for the great gift of the Broken Wheel ranch, which they would fill with the happy sound of children's laughter, and a whole lot of happy times.